FATE'S ATTRACTION

DIRK GREYSON

DREAMSPINNER
PRESS

Published by
DREAMSPINNER PRESS

5032 Capital Circle SW, Suite 2, PMB# 279,
Tallahassee, FL 32305-7886 USA
www.dreamspinnerpress.com

This is a work of fiction. Names, characters, places, and incidents either are the product of Dirk Greyson imagination or are used fictitiously, and any resemblance to actual persons, living or dead, business establishments, events, or locales is entirely coincidental.

Fate's Attraction
© 2021 Dirk Greyson

Cover Art
© 2021 L.C. Chase
http://www.lcchase.com
Cover content is for illustrative purposes only and any person depicted on the cover is a model.

Mass Market Paperback ISBN: 978-1-64108-236-5
Trade Paperback ISBN: 978-1-64405-877-0
Digital ISBN: 978-1-64405-876-3
Mass Market Paperback published August 2021
v. 1.1

Printed in the United States of America
∞
This paper meets the requirements of
ANSI/NISO Z39.48-1992 (Permanence of Paper).

Readers love DIRK GREYSON

Prey for Love

"*Prey for Love* is a well written suspense novel with decent emotional engagement, a fairly high trepidation factor, and a slow-burn romance."
—Rainbow Book Reviews

"For a suspenseful, hot, but occasionally funny read, pick this one up. What can be better than a smoking hot marine and friends and the people who love them?"
—Sparkling Book Reviews

Hell and Back

"*Hell and Back* is a stand-alone romance/thriller with plenty of action and a sizzling romance to keep you entertained and invested in its outcome."
—Divine Magazine

"This book is filled with suspense, betrayals and sex. It is a book about second chances and it is a search for secrets and staying alive."
—Paranormal Romance Guild

Lost Mate

"Do yourself a favor and pick up this book or anything that Mr. Greyson has written. You will not be sorry."
—Harlie Williams

By Dirk Greyson

An Assassin's Holiday
Fate's Attraction
Flight or Fight
Hell and Back
Lost Mate
Notes from Home
Playing With Fire
Prey for Love

DAY AND KNIGHT
Day and Knight
Sun and Shadow
Dawn and Dusk

YELLOWSTONE WOLVES
Challenge the Darkness
Darkness Threatening
Darkness Rising

Published by DREAMSPINNER PRESS
www.dreamspinnerpress.com

To Gin and Brenda for helping to make this story amazing.

CHAPTER 1

VLADIMIR CORELIA loved the woods. They were home—*his* home—and he knew them like the back of his hand. Every tree that formed the canopy overhead, the rocks, the stream that ran through the pack lands, gurgling as it rounded the bend before filling the swimming hole he and the other pups had played in as children—they were a part of him. His inner wolf longed to be released so he could run and play, maybe chase the squirrel that skittered across the leaves up ahead as it searched for nuts to store for winter.

"You know your father is going to have your head for being out this far," Ruck said, bursting out from behind one of the trees.

"I knew you were there. I've smelled you for the last half hour," Vladimir said, greeting his old friend. While technically this was still their pack land, Ralston Corelia, his father and alpha of the pack, insisted that pack members never venture this far. "What are you doing here? You know my father will hunt you down if he knows you're around." Not that Vladimir really cared what his father thought on the subject, but he didn't want Ruck to get hurt. He and Ruck had been friends for a long time.

Well. *Secret* friends.

"I know. Your father doesn't like bears," Ruck grumbled, propping one foot on a log that had fallen across the trail. "Even though we've been here just as long as you have and have lived beside each other without incident for hundreds of years." Ruck stood and went to a tree, scratching his back on the bark. "I hate wearing clothes. Maybe I should just go furry all the time and say to hell with it."

Vladimir knew the feeling. There were times he felt just as alone as Ruck, though at least he had a pack and people who tried to look after him. Not that Vladimir fit in with everyone else. He knew he was different, just like Ruck. Only Vladimir's difference was on the inside. So far he had been able to hide it, but that was only going to last so long. His father was already pushing she-wolves in his direction at an alarming rate, and it wouldn't be long before he figured out why Vladimir kept putting him off. He stood next to Ruck and leaned against him. "Maybe you should migrate to where there are other bears. You could find yourself a woman who was interested."

Ruck sighed. "Doesn't work that way for me any more than it does for you," he said. "And you know it." His laugh boomed out over the empty forest as he bumped Vlad's shoulder, nearly knocking him back. "So what brings you out all this way?"

"Maybe I just wanted to see you," Vlad answered, wondering for the millionth time why he and Ruck had never become more than just friends. It just wouldn't feel right. Granted, his father would have a shit fit of epic proportions, but eventually he'd have to get over it. It wasn't like he and Ruck were going to have children or anything. His best answer was that Vladimir loved Ruck the way he would a brother.... Actually, they were better than brothers, since his own was a complete piece of shit.

"Or you wanted to get far away from Dimitri and you knew he'd never come out here. That brother of yours is a real piece of work. Makes me glad I was an only child." Technically Ruck was an orphan. Both his parents had died a few years ago, leaving him alone in the world. Bears didn't tend to run in packs the way wolves did—Ruck had explained that they were largely solitary creatures—but it tore at Vlad's heart how alone Ruck was all the time.

Vlad figured he should change the subject. "Why are *you* here?"

"I smelled one of your kind and came to investigate. Then I ran into you and thought I'd figured it out, but it isn't that. There's someone else—multiple someones, if my nose is right. The scent comes and goes with the wind, and I've had a hard time narrowing it down. The breeze keeps changing direction and swirling through these hills in weird ways today."

Vlad jumped to his feet, surprised he didn't scent it himself. "Then we'd better find out what's going on. If other wolves have moved into our territory, there's going to be a fight. And you know Dimitri might stir things up and make them worse just to prove that he's worthy of becoming the next big wolf to take over." His brother would do anything to be the next alpha. Unfortunately, that meant acting in ways that were wrong, as far as Vlad was concerned. Their father didn't like his actions either.

Vladimir lifted his nose, scenting the air. Even in human form, his sense of smell was danged good. In wolf form, it was outstanding. But he didn't smell any-thing. "Where did you smell it last?"

Ruck tilted his head off to the north.

They walked together, knowing each other well enough that there was no need for constant chatter. "See?" Ruck asked, pausing, and Vlad got just a hint of the scent. The breeze shifted, scattering the hint on the trail, wiping it away once again. "Let's go farther this way."

Vlad stood still. "There it is," he whispered. As he followed the scent, it got stronger. He picked up his pace, the breeze stirring the smell, but he had it now, and it seemed Ruck did as well. "You're right, there are all kind of scents mixed together. I get human and wolf mixed, but also just wolf… and something else. It's like a soup—I can't tell exactly what's in it yet."

"Yeah," Ruck agreed. They continued on, follow-ing the olfactory trail through the forest.

"We're off pack land," Vladimir declared a few seconds later as they crossed the old boundary that marked the edge of their pack's territory. He continued forward. "I smell blood." He slowed, growing more cautious.

"Me too. It's fresh, but not immediate, I don't think," Ruck agreed.

The scent grew thicker and more pungent. Vladi-mir wrinkled his nose, wondering if he should simply tell Ruck to take off and be safe before he returned to the pack to take whatever licking his father chose to give him once he got help. He felt his own wolf's met-aphorical fur standing on end.

"It smells bad," Ruck said. "Everything inside me screams that something dark happened here." He paused beside a tree. "My bear wants out bad, and he wants to go the other way."

Vladimir nodded. His wolf felt the same, but Vladimir had to know what had happened. If this was something sinister and it had happened this close to pack land, then it was only a matter of time before it spilled over. That would be bad. "I've got your back and you've got mine." He steeled himself and cautiously continued forward as the scent grew stronger. The air hung under the trees, as if even the breeze didn't want to enter.

"Look," Ruck whispered. "There's something up ahead." He pointed, and Vladimir continued forward. "It's a wolf." He stopped. "You better handle this. He isn't going to know me, and who knows what will happen if he's still alive."

Vladimir skulked forward, barely near enough to see the wolf's chest rising and falling. He was close enough to know that the wolf was a shifter, and from the blood and cuts, Vladimir could tell he'd been attacked. "Ruck," Vladimir called, and his friend hurried forward. "This isn't good."

"Do you know this guy?" He wrinkled his nose. "He smells really off."

Vladimir shook his head, wondering why the wolf wasn't healing. Under normal circumstances, their bodies would begin to heal almost immediately. A shift usually repaired most damage, but this wolf had been injured and was probably too weak to shift. Vladimir checked him over, rolling the wolf onto his other side. "Shit." He covered his hand with his sleeve and pulled a small silver knife out of the wolf's side. That was the reason he wasn't healing. Hopefully now he'd begin to.

He dropped the blade to the forest floor. "I'll see if I can get some water. If we clean the wounds and get him something to drink, it might help." He got up but then thought again. "No. We can't split up. There's still something else. Where did this guy come from? The pack would have known if he'd been here very long. The patrols would have picked him up eventually." He lifted his nose, wishing he could take the chance to shift.

"That way. It's part of what I smelled earlier." Ruck headed off a short ways, and Vladimir looked for something to bind the wolf's wounds. He found nothing. "Vladimir," Ruck whispered. "Get over here."

Vlad carefully lifted the wolf into his arms, following the sound of Ruck's voice. "What is it?"

"A cave of some sort. And it's a big one. Do you think he'd been living in there? It smells wolfy. I'll stay here with him. You go check it out." Ruck took the wolf and cradled him in his arms.

Vladimir approached the cave entrance, scented for danger, then went inside.

Overlapping scents filled his nose: wolf, human, animal, bodily fluids, food—it was nearly overwhelming. Fortunately Vladimir could see well in the dark, since he only had the light of the cave mouth to see by. He took a few more steps and came to a larger room with a few blankets, boxes, and… stuff.

Four wolf cubs approached him cautiously. They had to be only about three or four weeks old. They were full-blooded wolves, and after some smelling and posturing, they came forward. Vladimir petted each of them, transferring his scent, letting them know that he wasn't going to hurt them. Once they knew they were safe, the three boys and the girl pup began to roughhouse and play, trying to pull him into their game. And they might have succeeded if not for a wail from the other side of the room.

A baby. Vladimir hurried over, with the pups right behind him, and lifted up the little one. The child was clearly a shifter like him, a few months old, but fat and healthy judging by the force of his scream. The kid was probably hungry, and sure enough, Vladimir found a box with bottles and formula, as well as a jug of water that he began heating on a tiny stove. They made the formula and set it in some cold water to cool.

He'd seen the parents of the pack make up bottles, so he did his best and popped the nipple into the little guy's mouth. He instantly quieted, sucking the nourishment like it was going out of style.

"What's happening?" Ruck asked from the mouth of the cave.

Vladimir wrapped the baby in a blanket and carried him out with him, the pups following. "I think we found out why this guy was here and what he was doing." Though the pups and the baby raised a lot more questions.

"Oh hell. What are we going to do?" he asked as the pups burst out of the cave behind Vladimir.

"I need to call for help." There was no other choice. His father was going to be totally pissed, but they didn't have a choice. "Is he at least healing?"

Ruck nodded and carefully set the wolf down.

"There are blankets and water inside. We can make him more comfortable."

Ruck nodded again and hurried inside. He returned with a blanket that he spread over the injured wolf. The cubs climbed on top of the blanket and lay next to the injured wolf, offering what comfort they could.

Vladimir gently handed the baby to Ruck, who continued feeding him while Vlad stripped off his clothes. He willed his body to reshape, bones repositioning, teeth lengthening, skin reforming—undergoing the change his kind had endured for thousands of years—until he stood on all fours, his senses even more attuned to the forest around him.

He inhaled, sensing more clearly the beings around him, knowing that the baby was settling in to sleep, its heartbeat steadying after the shock of being surrounded by strangers, the pups still on alert even as they curled near the injured wolf. Vladimir inhaled, tuning in to the injured stranger. Something about him drew his attention. His scent was off, probably from the silver, but it still drew Vladimir over everyone and everything else around him. It tickled his nose, and he had to force himself not to approach and smell him more closely. Vladimir had a job to do, and as much as he hated it, he needed the help of his pack and he hadn't thought to bring his cell.

He barked twice, short yips, and then bounded into the woods. He climbed one of the short hills, turned his head to the sky, and let out a cry to alert his father. Goddess help him and secure him from his father's anger. He was going to need it. He sure hoped his alpha didn't send Dimitri. That was the last thing Vladimir needed.

A cry answered him, and Vladimir called out once more before racing back to the others. Ruck still held the now-sleeping baby, rocking him slowly, the pups watching him, two hurrying over to nip at his legs, urging him to play. The injured wolf seemed to be gaining strength. His heart beat more strongly, and his breathing was deeper than before. As Vladimir drew closer, he could hear the blood coursing through him and smell the stranger's scent growing less muddled as his system dealt with the effects of the silver poisoning. His eyes remained closed.

"Do you want me to stay?" Ruck asked, shifting his weight from foot to foot. But Vladimir knew he had to face the consequences alone. They would scent Ruck, but if the pack found Ruck here, they would probably attack him before asking questions. He groaned in his head and triggered the shift back to human. By the time he stood naked in front of his friend, Vladimir could hardly remain upright. Two transitions in a short time took a lot of energy. He really needed to eat, but it didn't seem like that was going to happen any time soon.

"Give me the baby and head off. Get as far as you can, and mask your scent in the stream." He took the little guy, then watched Ruck disappear into the forest. The breeze, which had stayed away, probably out of its own fear of what had happened here, made a reappearance, following Ruck and taking some of his scent along with him. Vladimir took a minute to pull on his clothes.

"What…." Sasha burst from the trees in human form ten minutes later with Martha and Casimir. Sasha and Casimir were his father's two beta wolves, and Martha was Casimir's mate, and nearly as fierce as the others. If his father ever needed a third beta, it would be her.

"There's no danger," Vladimir said as they took in the scene. "But I do need a little help."

"Oh my goddess," Martha said as she hurried forward, her demeanor changing in an instant. "What have we here?" She approached and took the baby from him, her face lighting into a smile Vladimir had never seen from her. The rest of them, including her mate, exchanged glances at the change.

"You'd better explain what's going on," Sasha said, all business.

Vladimir relayed what little he knew. "The cave contains whatever supplies he had. It's my guess that he was trying to take care of the babe and came across the cubs and tried to help them too." He explained where they found the wolf. "But he wasn't attacked there. There are no signs of a struggle or blood. I think he was trying to get back to the cave when he passed out."

Sasha tilted his head to Casimir. "Go see if you can find out where he was attacked. Maybe that will tell us something about who did this, but be careful. I'm scenting a bear in the area. Maybe that's the source of the trouble."

Vladimir bit his lower lip as he finished dressing. "The injuries on him are from a wolf and that." He pointed to the silver knife. "This was done by someone who knows about wolves and our weakness. It wasn't from a bear or a random hunter. This was done intentionally." And that was what bothered Vladimir the most—that it was done by one of their own.

"We need to get everyone back. This isn't our land," Sasha said as Casimir returned. "Find anything?"

"A clearing a little ways off. It smelled strange," he shivered. "Like…."

"Dark, black, and cold?" Vladimir supplied, putting words to his feelings, and Casimir nodded. "Something bad happened there." He turned his attention to the injured wolf. "I don't know what, but we should get out of here and try to help him. Maybe he'll be able to tell us what's going on when he wakes up."

Sasha nodded and organized them all. Martha carried the baby, and Sasha bent down to pick up the injured wolf. Vladimir's wolf growled and he batted Sasha away, baring his teeth at him. Sasha growled in return.

"Stop it, Sasha," Martha snapped, and Vladimir lifted the wolf into his arms, cradling him gently in the blanket. "Get the pups and bring whatever he was using to feed the baby. We need to get out of here without any more bloodshed." She lifted her head and scented the air. "I don't like this place at all."

"Me neither," Casimir agreed as he returned with a blanket that he gathered the pups into, settling them as best he could for the trip back. They tried to climb out until he growled gently and bared his teeth. Then they grew quiet so he could carry them.

They made quite a caravan through the woods, which grew lighter and weighed less heavily on Vladimir's spirit the farther away they got from the cave.

"What were you doing out there?" Sasha asked. "You know your father is furious that you were there against his orders… again." He was lugging the box of formula as well as a bundle of belongings.

"He's never happy with me anyway, so why worry about it now?" Vladimir argued. "He doesn't like anything I do and he watches me constantly. Do you have any idea how stifling it is when I can't even take a walk without him wanting to send someone with me? As if I'm not strong enough to take care of myself?" Vladimir just wanted to have a life of his own and to be able to make his own decisions rather than having them made for him all the time. Was that too much to ask? He didn't think so. But to his father, you'd think he wanted the world and everything in it.

He grew quiet, watching the path ahead and making sure he didn't jostle the injured wolf he carried.

"You know your father just wants to protect you," Martha said as she walked next to him. They had to move much more slowly than normal.

"I know. Everyone thinks I'm weak just because I'm smaller than them," Vladimir grumbled. It was the usual thing. Out in the woods, alone, he could be who he truly was, without being fussed over because he wasn't as strong as other wolves his age. Worse, Vladimir's place in the pack was a source of consternation to his super virile and powerful father. He figured he'd have children who were as powerful as he was so he could groom them to take over the pack. Instead, the pack's alpha got a runt for a second son whom he had to watch over all the time.

"You are who you are, Vladimir," she said softly.

"Exactly. But no one will just let me be that person. I have to try to be who they want me to be, and sometimes that chafes." He stopped as the wolf in his arms began to move. "It's okay," he said to the wolf in a soft tone. "You're safe. I'm taking you to get some help. Just relax. I'm helping you." He picked up his pace, and they approached the compound just as the wolf opened his eyes.

"We need the healer now," Sasha told one of the boys playing a game with friends, who raced off through the opening between the small set of rustic homes. The pack lived simply and close to the land the way they always had, keeping a low profile and doing their best to avoid the notice of the outside world farther to the south and east.

"Bring them all to my cabin," Vladimir said, and the others followed him. Vladimir opened the door and set the wolf on the small bed against the wall. The others followed him in.

"I'll get something for these little guys to eat," Casimir offered after placing the pups on the floor. They hurried off to explore, and he left the cabin.

"Do you think he's going to be okay?" Vladimir asked Martha once the others had left. "He opened his eyes on the way back, but now he's not responding again." His wolf paced inside him, and Vladimir had no idea why he was so agitated. He felt his wolf pushing at his control, almost throwing himself at Vladimir to get out.

"Raisa will be here soon, and she'll know what to do," Martha said, still cradling the baby as though she never wanted to let him go.

"I can take him," Vladimir offered, but she ignored him, sitting in the chair next to the table. "He's going to need to be changed." He wasn't sure what to do, but Martha seemed to know. She located some diapers in the bundle of things from the cave and easily changed him while he rested on her outstretched legs. "You'll make a good mother." She clearly wanted children and was good with them. Vladimir had wondered why she and Casimir never had children as he got a basin of water.

She shook her head. "The goddess doesn't see that in my future," she finally answered. He swallowed at the hurt in her voice but wasn't sure what to say or do to help. Vladimir wrinkled his nose at the scent from the diaper, but Martha rolled it up and handed it to him. "Just put it outside and I'll dispose of it when I leave." She washed the baby and gasped when she rolled the little boy on his side. "Look." She pointed to a cherry-red mark above his hip, shaped like a crescent.

"What?" He leaned closer.

"The mark of darkness," she explained.

Vladimir crossed his arms. "Do you really believe those things? He's just a baby." Sometimes people got the strangest notions. "It looks like the moon to me, and that's always been good luck for us."

A groan came from the bed. Vladimir left Martha and dealt with the diaper, then hurried over just as Raisa came into the cabin.

"Everyone out of the way," she demanded.

Vladimir growled at her as he sat on the side of the bed, his wolf ready to pounce.

"Vladimir," she said, gentling her tone. Then she scented the air for a second and paused, looking at each of them. "I need to see in order to help." She approached more slowly, and Vladimir scooted low on the bed but refused to move away while she bent over the wolf. "I see you're awake but weak," she said to the wolf as she looked over the wounds. "You're healing, but it's going to take a while because of the silver." She put her hand on the wolf's head and held it there for a few seconds before pulling away.

"What are you going to do?" Vladimir asked. "You need to help him."

She patted his cheek the way she'd done when he'd been an impatient pup. "His body is doing what it needs to already. Give him some time to build his strength. Then he can change back." She straightened up. "Do you have any idea who he is?"

Vladimir shook his head.

Raisa paused. "I know you don't know his name, but are you aware of what he is to you?" She intensely searched Vladimir's gaze, and he shrugged.

"I guess he's someone I need to take care of, since I rescued him," Vladimir answered, unsure what sort of answer Raisa expected. Had she smelled something?

"Honey," Martha said gently, "what Raisa is asking is if you realize that this man is your mate?" Martha could be one hell of a badass, but she was also always kind to him. Since his mother had died some time ago, she was the closest thing to a mother figure he had, even if she wasn't that much older than him.

Vladimir tilted his head to the side, inhaling deeply. The wolf's scent tickled his nose. It had changed, and now it went through him like a falling tree crashing to the ground. Vladimir's cock hardened in an instant, and all he wanted was more of that summer rain and clean woods scent. "I don't understand." He had never given a mate a second thought. "But…."

Martha rocked the baby in her arms as he stirred, and she made up a bottle, then fed it to him before he started fussing in earnest. "I know there are people like your father who believe that wolves like you, those who are drawn to the same sex, don't get mates."

"A bunch of poppycock, if you ask me," Raisa said. "The proof is right in this room. I can scent both their excitements." Raisa had been around long enough that she didn't mince words, even if it wasn't polite to mention such things.

Vladimir did his best to prevent himself from shaking. He didn't want the others to see his fear, but that was futile. They could smell it on him—or would, in a matter of seconds. Vladimir sat taller, looking at the wolf in his bed, surprised at how right this all felt. "What do I do?"

The pups all gathered around his feet, and Vladimir lifted them up one by one. They settled around the wolf, forming a puppy pile and curling up to sleep.

"Let him sleep for now. There is little else we can do until he's strong enough to shift back. In the meantime, I'll bring something for the pups, and Martha can care for the baby." She patted Vladimir's shoulder. "It will be all right."

"But the alpha…," Vladimir whispered. He knew there was no convincing his father. He was a good alpha, strong and protective of the pack. Vladimir knew that. But his father had his opinions, and he adhered to tradition and the old ways. He was slow to change and rarely if ever admitted that he was wrong… at least, not since Vladimir's mother died.

Raisa and Martha shared a brief look that told Vladimir all he needed to know. He was on his own as far as his father went.

Casimir returned with a bowl of water that he placed on the floor and some cooked ground meat. The pups jumped off the bed as soon as they smelled the food and raced over, yipping and shuffling to get at it.

"Your father wants to see you as soon as you're done here," he said.

Vladimir sighed.

"Go see him. Raisa and I will stay here until you get back," Martha told him.

So Vladimir followed Casimir out of his cabin. He crossed the pack compound before entering the larger main pack house.

His grandparents had built the building, and it was where Vladimir had grown up. His mother had redecorated the common rooms, adding large windows that overlooked the pack compound as well as the hills at the back of the house, so that at pack gatherings, every-one could see the thick surrounding greenery. Vladimir always loved how the windows brought the outside in, as did the wide plank flooring, log walls, and plank ceilings.

"Vlad," his father snapped, pulling him out of his momentary trip down memory lane. "Come in here." He stood at the door to his office.

Vladimir took a deep breath then entered the room.

His father closed the door behind him. "I'm very disappointed in you. I can't begin to—"

"What? I rescued a fellow wolf shifter, not to mention a baby, as well as a litter of wolf cubs. Dad—a litter of natural wolf cubs! There haven't been any wolves—real wolves—in these hills in a long time. Grandpa always told me that we were the only ones left out here."

His father slammed his hand on the top of the desk. "You know damned well what I'm talking about. That area is off-limits for a reason. There have been dark things happening out there."

"Yeah, so you're going to turn your back on them? We have to figure out what's going on. Besides, I was just out there to go swimming like I did when I was a kid."

"You aren't a kid any longer, and I don't make decisions for my own health. I do it to keep the pack safe." His father's intense gaze bored holes into Vladi-mir, and he felt his resistance fading.

"No, I'm not a kid. But we should all feel safe to wander beyond pack lands." He sat in one of the rough-hewn chairs, not staring back, because his dad would see that as a challenge. Still, he thought his dad was being shortsighted. "And I did feel something dark out there—so did the others. Someone was attacked—with silver. And you know that kind of violence leaves a stain."

His dad didn't back down for an instant. It wasn't like Vladimir expected him to. "And Casimir and Sasha said they smelled a bear. I'm going to send a party out to find and remove that kind of threat."

"There is no threat," Vladimir said. "Other than whoever nearly killed the wolf who is in my cabin. That's the real threat. We should be figuring out what happened." He didn't want to tell his father about Ruck, but he couldn't have the pack hunting him down either. "The bear is a friend. Okay? I've known him a long time, and he didn't do this." His father's face grew red, and Vladimir knew he was going to blow any second. "Can you just listen to someone else for two seconds? You don't know everything." Vladimir was getting so angry, he could hardly sit still.

"I'm your alpha, and it's my job to make decisions for the safety of the entire pack and—"

"Then make them, Dad. But get all the facts first," Vladimir said more calmly. Arguing with his father wasn't going to get him anything. His dad's ego would rise, and any defiance would be seen as a challenge to his Dirk Greysonity. "I've known Ruck for a long time. He lives outside of our territory and watches over things. You remember that possible incursion of mountain lions a few years ago? The ones we fought off because we found out early? Ruck was the one who told me about them." He had to come clean if he wanted any chance of his father leaving his friend alone. "I know he didn't attack the wolf."

His father growled deep in his throat, but Vladimir knew that was the way his father vocalized the fact that he hadn't been right. "Fine. If you say so. But if that bear comes wandering close to the pack, I'll take action. And as for this injured wolf, he's your responsibility, as are these pups and the baby."

Vladimir nodded. "I think Martha has taken over care of the baby."

For the first time he could remember, his father's expression truly softened, and there was pain visible behind his eyes. Vladimir never saw emotion from his father. He always projected an air of strength and confidence. "She's wanted a baby for quite some time."

Vladimir nodded slowly. Now her reaction made sense. If she and Casimir hadn't been able to have pups…. "She seems to know what to do, and the boy is taken with her."

His father cleared his throat. "You are still responsible for the rest of what you have brought to the pack. Watch over our injured wolf and find out if he's friend or foe. Just because he lost the fight, that doesn't mean he isn't the one who started it or isn't the source of the darkness you felt. I won't have the pack threatened." He stepped closer, looming over Vladimir. "And in the future, you will obey my orders. They are there to keep you and the rest of the pack safe. Understand?" His father's bared teeth lengthened, a display of power and control. "I will not have any dissension in the pack, especially from one of my sons." He turned away and went behind his desk. "Go check on this wolf and try not to get into any more trouble." Then he dismissed Vladimir with a wave of his hand.

CHAPTER 2

FRANKIE SLOWLY became more and more aware of himself. His mind was still a stirring mass of disjointed thoughts and feelings, but things were coming back into focus. He was aware that he was in wolf form, but he didn't have the energy to lift his tail, let alone shift. He cracked his eyes open, but they didn't want to stay that way. Even looking around took too much energy. He felt as if he was in a fog that kept trying to cover him and pull him back under. Frankie resisted, forcing his eyes to open. He needed to know where he was and what had happened to him.

At least he was warm and not sleeping on the ground.

"Are you awake?" a masculine voice asked quietly.

Frankie couldn't answer in this form and didn't have the energy to, even if he could have. All he did was lie there and try to focus on something around him. Why was he here? He kept running all that through his mind. He knew his name but very little else. He tried to remember where he'd been before this and what he'd done to end up in this situation, but his mind was a blank. He recalled very basic things about himself, but that was all.

"Are you thirsty?" Water appeared in front of him, and Frankie used his last reserve of energy to move enough to be able to drink. His throat hurt as the water hit it, but then it soothed and went down. He drank more and then settled his head on the warm bed again. Frankie's eyes felt heavy once more, so he let them close. There was nothing more he could do. Even drinking that little bit of water had worn him out.

"I'm here and you aren't alone." A hand touched his head, caressing him gently, reassuring him that everything was indeed going to be okay.

Victor…. The name flashed through his mind, and he snapped his eyes open again. Where was Victor? He didn't hear him crying or fussing. Agitation ran through him and he lifted his head, listening. He tried scenting, but everything was so muddled that he couldn't process much. Frankie shook, which drained him of even more energy. He was helpless, and so was Victor. He needed to find him. Was he still back at the cave? How long had he been here? Was Victor even still alive? Frankie had no idea. His breathing became faster, and he panted, trying to get off the bed. He needed to find him, to get back to him.

"It's okay, relax. Everything is fine," the pleasant voice said. "The pups are sleeping next to you, and the baby is fine. A friend is looking after him. Just relax. You were stabbed with a silver knife, and it's going to take some time for the effects to leave your body."

That explained why he was so tired and didn't seem to be healing as quickly as he usually did. Under normal circumstances, his wounds should have healed on their own and he should be able to shift and finish the healing process. At least, he thought so. His memory was scattered, so maybe the whole healing thing was just some outlandish notion.

"Close your eyes and rest. I'll be here to make sure nothing happens to you." The voice was warm and soft, and Frankie closed his eyes once again, letting healing sleep take him.

WHEN FRANKIE woke again, he had more energy. His eyes weren't as heavy, and he could move his head without disorientation. He was alone on the bed but heard the scampering of light footsteps nearby, as well as soft yips and growls. Frankie opened his eyes to see the four pups wrestling on the floor just in front of him. He watched them, his mind racing. He remembered some of what happened before he was attacked, but it also seemed like there were huge blank spaces. Frankie knew that he'd rescued the four pups a few weeks ago after their mother had been killed, and that he'd brought them back to the cave to care for them.

He lifted his head, grateful the room didn't spin.

"You must be feeling better."

Frankie turned toward the voice. A man sat in a rustic chair with a book on his lap. He had dark blond hair and bright eyes, and when he smiled, Frankie thumped his tail against the bedding. He knew instinctively that this was his mate, and was tempted to jump down to get closer. But that was a bad idea. Frankie barely knew who this guy was, and he had so many things to worry about right now. How could he possibly claim a mate when he didn't know a lot about himself? All he could hope for was that the blank sections of his mind would fill in eventually. He sure as heck hoped so.

"Do you want to try to shift back? Are you hungry?" the man asked.

Frankie *was* hungry, and maybe that was a good sign. He wasn't sure he had the energy to shift back yet, but he needed to try. At least then he could talk and ask questions. Right now his mind swirled with things he needed to know but had no way to ask.

Frankie closed his eyes and tried to picture himself with feet and hands. He lay there as still as he could, but nothing happened. Panting, he rested his head back on the bedding. He didn't have enough energy to shift yet. Just the effort wore him out, and he closed his eyes once more.

There was nothing he could do until he could shift back. Only then would he get some answers. Unfortunately, it seemed a lot of those answers had to come from him. But right now he had no idea what they were.

"THERE YOU are," the man said quietly sometime later.

This time when Frankie woke, he was more lucid. The darkness over parts of his memory was still there, but at least he could think clearly, and when he lifted his head, he didn't feel as if he had to go right back to sleep.

"Feeling better? I have some water and a little food, if you're hungry."

At the mention of food, Frankie's belly rumbled, and he tried to stand. His legs were wobbly for a few seconds but then steadied, and he was able to climb down to the floor. Though he was still weak, he was able to walk around the small space. That was an improvement. The pups raced around him, trying to get Frankie to play, but he wasn't up for that.

"Do you want to try to shift back?" the man asked.

Frankie nodded and then concentrated, trying to connect with his human form. It seemed elusive, though, like whatever he was trying to find was just out of reach. He knew it was there, but as much as he concentrated on taking human form, he stayed the way he was.

"Maybe you need to eat and get stronger."

Or maybe whatever he needed was hidden in those blank parts of his mind. That thought was frightening, and Frankie wished he could connect with that other part of him so he could change back. There were so many questions, and this man with him, his mate, had to have just as many. Frankie lifted his gaze, comparing this man to anyone in his limited memory, but came up empty. He wished he knew the guy's name.

As if he could read Frankie's mind, the man said, "I'm Vladimir. And from the name in the notebook we found in the cave, I'm going to guess that you're Frankie. At least I hope so. I put your stuff over there by the bed. You can go through it later when you're feeling better. But I needed to know what to call you." He smiled and sat down on the floor next to Frankie, and the pups all ran over to him and piled into his lap. "Let me see what I can tell you. I found you injured in the forest. I think you were in a fight of some sort—I pulled out a silver knife from your back. It wasn't big, but it might have been there awhile. We aren't sure, but Raisa, our healer, says you got a bad case of silver poisoning and that's why it's taking so long for you to heal." He got up from the floor, the pups scattering, and put down some water and held out a plate of meat to

Frankie. "I don't dare put it down or these four will be all over it." As it was, the pups jumped at the plate.

Frankie growled a warning, and the pups settled down. They were familiar enough with him and his scent that they weren't afraid of him, but they knew enough to obey, at least for a few minutes, giving Frankie a chance to eat a little before the rascals were back. Vladimir put another bowl on the floor, and the four of them scampered over to it while Frankie finished his meal.

"I don't want you to eat too much too fast. Martha said she would bring some more in a little while. She's also going to bring the baby back so you can see him." Vladimir stroked his head and down his back. Frankie drew closer, rubbing against him. He needed some sort of reassurance, and Vladimir was his mate. Damn... it figured. He'd met his mate and he was stuck in wolf form. Granted, Vladimir could shift too, but at least one of them needed to have opposable thumbs and the ability to communicate. Frankie huffed and lay down on the floor, already tired, only this time it felt more like it came from contentment and having a full belly than sheer fatigue.

Vladimir kept in contact with him, his hand on his back. The pups finished eating and raced over, wanting to play, but thankfully they settled down right near him and snuggled in. If Frankie let himself dream, he could easily imagine them as some sort of weird family. But just that thought was enough to send him into a grief spiral. The loss was still so new—and unfortunately for him, he remembered every part of it. Maybe it was a good thing he wasn't in human form. Otherwise his mate would see him fall apart. As it was, he closed his eyes and tried not to let the loss of his family, the life he once knew, overtake him. Maybe it was best if he escaped in sleep. Only that didn't seem to be in the cards.

"How is he?" a woman asked as she entered.

Frankie cracked his eyes open, smelling Victor instantly. He stood and walked over to the woman. When she sat down, Frankie nudged Victor with his nose.

"The little man is doing well." She set Victor on her lap, and Frankie sniffed the baby all over, just to make sure he was okay. Victor was the only family he had left. It had taken all his skill and some luck to get him away safely—everyone else was gone—and he was relieved the baby was being so well cared for. Not that Frankie could do much for him in this state.

Frankie licked her hand once in thanks and then went to the bed and curled into a ball at the bottom. There was nothing anyone could do for him now. His life had been turned upside down, and while he had needed help at the time, all he'd been able to do was disappear into the woods to wait it out. But what he'd been running from, he still had no idea.

"I take it he still isn't able to shift back," the woman said.

"No. I think it's the silver. At least that's what I'm hoping it is. I asked Raisa about it, but she says we need to be patient, that it will take time for the silver to totally leave his system." Vladimir sounded as concerned as Frankie felt. "How is this little guy?"

"He outeats my mate and poops like a trooper, then he sleeps and wakes up hungry." She seemed subdued. Judging by the power that rolled off her, that was probably an unusual occurrence.

"Martha, are you okay?" Vladimir asked. Now, at least, Frankie knew her name.

"I will be," she said, cradling Victor in her arms. "Casimir and I have been trying for pups for four years with nothing to show for it. Nothing at all. I think maybe I can't have them. Raisa says that there is something stuck inside me, but I have no idea what that means. You know how she can be enigmatic at times."

They both grew quiet, and Frankie closed his eyes, figuring he might as well rest. Maybe once he woke up again, his memory would be clearer and whatever was stopping him from shifting would have worked its way out.

"HE ISN'T able to shift," Vladimir said quietly as Frankie returned to consciousness. "He's tried a couple of times and it just won't happen."

The forceful presence of an alpha had Frankie getting up and climbing off the bed to greet him and bare his neck in respect.

The alpha nodded in acknowledgment. "Do we know anything about him?"

"His name is Franklin Bowers, and he was taking care of the baby and the wolf cubs just off pack land," Vladimir explained and stepped back.

The alpha came closer, leaning down to look into Frankie's eyes. Frankie lowered his gaze slightly but didn't turn away. If the alpha thought he'd find something, Frankie wasn't going to hide it.

"I'm Alpha Corelia, and you're on my pack land. We need to know why you are here and what happened to you."

Yeah, Frankie would like to know that too. He remembered being attacked but not who had been behind it. That part of his memory was a huge blank.

"The babe is fine, strong, and eating well," the alpha continued. He pulled back slightly and then rubbed his hand against Frankie, transferring scent.

A sense of calm that Frankie hadn't felt in quite some time washed over him. He had been doing his best for Victor and the wolf cubs, but it had all been very overwhelming. It was nice to have someone strong to lean on, someone who would take charge. He'd never been one of those wolves who wanted to run things. He was content to be part of a pack and contribute to the well-being of the group. He leaned into the touch, rubbing against the alpha, who seemed satisfied with the response.

"Rest. We'll talk once you're able to shift again." He drew away and motioned for Vladimir to follow him out. The pups raced along, following the alpha wolf out the door.

Frankie had found the litter of pups near the stream, cold, huddled together, and near death. Their mother should have been close by, but he had watched for hours, and she didn't return. Frankie had tried to find her but had no luck and ended up feeding the pups some of Victor's formula to try to keep them alive. Once they were old enough, he hunted for them while Victor was asleep in the cave. For weeks his life had been about keeping the charges in his care safe and the specter of death that seemed to stalk them at bay. Those sorts of things he remembered, but others, like how he was injured and what his life had been like before he ended up in the cave, seemed to have vanished.

Frankie lay down, waiting for Vladimir to return. He could hear voices drifting in through the door and made out a few words, but not enough to understand what was being talked about.

When Vladimir returned, he didn't seem happy. He closed the door with more force than necessary. The pups came in as well and raced over to Frankie. He nudged each of them and lay down on the rug off to the side.

He felt helpless, and that really sucked. Trapped in this form, he couldn't ask the questions that kept churning in his mind or answer any of the ones Vladimir and the alpha had for him. Stuck. Frankie was stuck, and the question that kept running through his head was... for how long?

CHAPTER 3

"ARE YOU sure he still isn't able to shift? It seems like he's strong enough," Vladimir's father asked yet again a few days later.

"You met him. Did he seem like he was lying to you?" Vladimir responded. His father prided himself on being a good judge of other wolves, and Vladimir used that against him a little. "He's getting stronger, but every time he tries to shift, all I sense is frustration."

The office door flew open and Dimitri burst in. "What is this stranger doing in the compound? And these wolf pups...."

Their father didn't answer. "Where have you been?"

"Hunting." He flashed a smirk at Vladimir. "I brought back two deer for the pack." The self-satisfaction in his eyes made Vladimir want to disappear. He knew he was a disappointment to his father. How many times had the alpha asked him why he couldn't be more like Dimitri? Vladimir had lost count years ago.

"Good. We have more mouths to feed. Your brother found a wolf in the woods who needs our help." His father and brother stared at each other.

Dimitri broke first, tilting his head slightly.

"At least I wasn't wandering around areas that were off-limits," Dimitri said, as though he was the perfect son who always did everything right. Vladimir knew better. Dimitri was always good when their father was around, but the minute the alpha's back was turned, he did exactly what he wanted. And somehow he never got caught. When they were kids, Dimitri used to blame Vladimir for any of his antics that got out of hand, and sure enough, Vlad would be punished every time.

"Stop being a jerk," Vladimir tossed back at him. He was tired of Dimitri's jabs. Not that he could do much about it. Dimitri had a good fifty pounds on him and was a wall of muscle. Pack life was all about power and strength. Vladimir had neither, at least physically.

"Both of you, knock it off," their father snapped. "I'm tired of the bickering." The alpha leaned over his desk. "Vladimir found a shifter who needs our care, along with a baby. And yes, the wolf pups. All of them have been given shelter in our pack. I don't need to say anything more. My decision has been made. Dimitri, take your game so it can be prepared."

"But father... we barely have enough to feed ourselves. Why are you bothering with a weak wolf and a bunch of mouths who will never contribute anything? They'll drain what few resources we have." He stood and stalked out of the office.

Vladimir stood as well. "I'm going to check on Frankie. Raisa looks in on him every day, but she has no idea why he isn't able to shift either. I'll do what I can."

His father seemed as puzzled as the rest of them. "Thank you," he said absently, and Vladimir took the opportunity to get out of the office before his father changed his mind.

"Vladimir," Martha called as she hurried up to him.

"Is something wrong with the baby?" he asked at her concerned expression.

"What? No. Casimir is watching him." She took him by the arm, leading him away from the others. "I was out by the creek, and I think I ran into a friend of yours. He was fishing but hurried away when I approached. I recognized his scent from the other day and realized he's a shifter."

Vladimir nodded. "His name's Ruck. He generally stays off pack land, but he watches the surrounding territory." He figured he might as well come clean with her. Martha listened and didn't rush to judgment, unlike others. Vladimir watched as Dimitri strode across the compound. "Ruck is a good guy, but he's a loner and doesn't understand pack stuff."

"I think you might want to take a walk out that way," Martha prompted, watching Dimitri as well. "Maybe take your mate with you. Get him out of the cabin and compound. Some fresh air might help him."

"What about the pups?" Vladimir asked. They needed to be watched. The four of them had a great deal of energy, and when they became bored, they got curious and could be destructive... as he'd found out with his second pair of shoes.

"We can keep an eye on them," Martha offered. "Go on." She rolled her eyes at him, and Vladimir figured he'd better not wait around for her to change her mind. He hurried back to the cabin and found Frankie pacing the floor.

"Let's get out of here," Vladimir told him, and Frankie bounded after him, clearly tired of being indoors. The pups followed them out, and Vladimir closed the door. The pack kids surrounded the pups, ready to play. Vladimir nodded his thanks to Martha as he and Frankie headed off into the woods.

The forest was new to Frankie, and Vladimir watched as he explored, trying to get to know his new environment. There were a ton of smells to discover, and Frankie bounded from place to place. He seemed happy—Vladimir could feel it, even though they hadn't permanently bonded yet. That wasn't something Vladimir was willing to do while Frankie was in wolf form, so they didn't have the kind of connection most mates in the pack had. It wasn't as intense or as strong, but that would change once Frankie could shift.

What if he's never able to shift? Vladimir asked himself. He'd tried not to think about it, but he was worried.

Frankie raced back to him, jumping through the ferns that covered the forest floor until he came up next to Vladimir and brushed against him. "I know," Vladimir said, pausing in his walk. "I probably should have shifted. But we're going to meet a friend at the stream. He was with me when I found you, and I'm hoping he might have discovered something. Ruck is a bear shifter, and I know he's going to smell different, but he's a good person and my friend." He thought it best to warn Frankie. "You can play if you want."

Frankie dropped his tail and continued to walk beside him, rubbing occasionally to transfer scent. Vladimir liked that his mate wanted to stay with him, though this had to be one of the strangest matings he had ever heard of. Vladimir felt the call to be with his mate all the time. His heart beat faster whenever he scented him, and his wolf grew more and more excited. He had shifted into wolf form so they could be together, and the last few nights they had slept that way, curled around each other. But that posed its own difficulties.

Frankie stopped all of a sudden, pointing, his entire body rigid. Vladimir inhaled and smiled. "That's Ruck. It's okay. He's a friend and helped me find you." Vladimir continued forward while Frankie moved more slowly and tensely, lifting each paw and putting it down again as though he were stalking prey.

"Hi, Vladimir," Ruck said as he emerged from the trees wearing only a pair of ragged shorts, his exposed barrel chest covered in red hair.

"Hi, Ruck. This is Frankie. He's the wolf we rescued the other day."

Ruck narrowed his eyes. "Does he want to stay in wolf form?"

"He can't shift back. We think the silver is interfering with his ability to shift, but we aren't sure." Vladimir placed his hand gently on Frankie's neck. "He's my mate."

Now it was Ruck's turn to be surprised. "I see." He sighed. "I know you wolves have mates, and when you find them, you stay with them for life. Bears don't have that. We tend to have a 'mate for now' sort of mentality." He looked the two of them over.

"Martha said you've been fishing a lot," Vladimir said. He wasn't sure what to talk about. Usually he and Ruck just talked, but things seemed different now.

"Yeah. I tried downstream, but there's something happening there. It doesn't feel right," he whispered. "It feels like it did the day we found *him*." He nodded at Frankie. "There's a dark oppression that hangs in the air. I don't know what it is, but it's getting stronger and it's heading for your land. They want something."

"Who?"

"I don't know. It's just a feeling. Maybe we should go over there and try to find out. But I don't want to go alone. Who or whatever they are, it's growing… and getting stronger." He shivered, and Vladimir didn't think it was from the cold.

"But what do we do?" Vladimir asked.

Frankie nudged his hand, agitated, and turned back the way they came. He paced along the path and came back, then walked back toward the pack compound.

"I think we have to figure out what the source of this darkness is. I know that seems like a weird way to describe it, but it's the feeling I get. Like something bad is going to happen," Ruck said. "There's a threat to all of us, and I can't fight it alone. I think it's too big for that. But I don't know anything about it."

Vladimir nodded. He didn't either. But Ruck was right, they had to know. This could affect the entire pack and his family, everyone he loved. Vladimir understood that a menace was threatening, but he didn't know what the source was. He'd come in contact with the darkness when he'd rescued Frankie, the pups, and the baby. He'd known he had to get them away from that, but if it was getting closer to the pack's lands, it had to be stopped. But how did you stop something you didn't know the source of?

"Is it human? I didn't smell anything that could tell me about who or what attacked Frankie. Nothing. Could the blood have covered up the scent? I don't know. But what there was to smell wasn't human."

"Was it a wolf?" Ruck asked. "Would a wolf have known how to disguise their scent from another wolf?" He sat down on a stump, and Vladimir sat next to him with Frankie resting at his feet, his side touching Vlad's leg. "I don't know. I don't think that this *thing* is some kind of ghost or devil or anything. Though it smells bad and hurts everything around it, I think it's something like you and me. Something that can be killed. But to do that, we have to know what it is."

"Did you ever hear any stories? There are some I heard when I was a pup about a wolf who went rogue after he was kicked out of his pack. He couldn't take it and went crazy, returning and killing everyone in the pack. He came at night with silver and flame, burning and murdering until they were all dead. Then he disappeared into the forest. Now it's said that he haunts it, watching for anyone he might coax over to his side." Vladimir shivered because he remembered Mama telling him that story. He'd thought it was something she'd said to make sure he was good and didn't wander away. It had worked.

Ruck shook his head. "We don't have stories like that. Mama raised us and taught us how to survive, but when we were old enough, it was up to us to go out in the world and find our own way. I spent a lot of my time alone. Ain't never met another bear shifter since."

Frankie grew agitated and began prowling.

"Is something out there?" Vladimir asked, scenting the air but not sensing anything.

Frankie walked over to Ruck, placed his front paws on his legs, and then hurried off down the path a short way before returning.

"Do you want us to follow you?"

Frankie shook his head, obviously trying to communicate.

"Do you know who attacked you?"

Another head shake.

"I wish you could talk to us."

Frankie lay down with a huff, his nose on his paws.

Ruck turned to Vladimir. "All I know is that the scent from the north keeps growing. Something or someone is on the move and they're coming this way, searching to see who's out here. I think they might have attacked Frankie because he got too close to them. I think it was humans, but I don't know why. It isn't the time of year they can hunt; you know that. But maybe they want something else."

"We'll have to go looking for them, then," Vladimir said. "See what it is they are after and what they look like." It was the only choice they had if they were going to keep the pack and their homes safe. "When do you want to do it?"

"It's going to storm tomorrow," Ruck said, as though it were obvious. Vladimir didn't have that kind of ability, but he knew Ruck well enough not to question his instincts. "Let's go the day after. But we need to do it during the day. I don't want to be out in that section of the woods at night. There are too many unknowns."

"Okay. I'll try to get away. My father has been watching me. He was pretty angry about me being out by the cave… though he did take my side, to a degree at least, when Dimitri gave me grief. I'll tell him that Frankie and I are going hunting or something." Vladimir looked upward. The sun was well past its zenith, sinking behind the trees. "I should get back. The pups are going to need feeding."

"Are you sure you want to do this?" Ruck asked.

"Yeah. I need to do something to prove to the pack that I'm not useless. They all think I can't take care of myself or anyone else. My father thinks I'm too small to trust with any responsibility. And my brother never fails to remind me that I'm not built like a brick shithouse the way he is." Vladimir got to his feet and paced a little through the clearing. "Everyone still treats me like a kid. Well, I'll show them. I'll figure out what's going on. Then I can make the pack safer." He paused and turned to Ruck. "I'll meet you here first thing in the morning day after tomorrow. Then we can go see what's going on."

"Okay. I'll look for you then." Ruck stood and headed for the stream. "Just be careful, okay?" He waded into the stream and walked to the far side, then disappeared into the woods.

As Vladimir was trying to figure out his next move, clouds slipped over the sun, darkening the sky. "We better get back," he told Frankie. They headed toward home with the sky darkening quickly behind them. "I can't remember the last time a storm came up this fast."

Frankie ran faster, with Vladimir right behind him, the wind rising, leaves blowing down around them. This was going to be some storm. He hoped they got back to the compound in time to help everyone batten down before it hit full force. Whatever was going on, this wasn't a good omen.

"Vladimir," Casimir said as soon as the two of them broke into the clearing. "Put the storm shutters on the windows. Then you need to get the pups and come to the pack house. Alpha wants everyone there before this thing hits." He raced off, and Vladimir hurried over with Frankie right behind him.

It was going to be bad—Vladimir could feel it in his bones. He hoped Ruck was okay but figured he had been out there on his own long enough that he knew what he was doing. Still, he would have felt much better if Ruck were here too. Yeah, his dad would have a fit and a half, but then his friends would all be together.

"Can you round up the pups?" Vladimir asked Frankie. After rubbing his head against Vladimir's leg, he took off. The gesture was gentle and intimate. Vladimir hoped that no one else saw it, because he wanted it to be just for him. It was so strange having a mate, especially when they were in two different forms. Maybe once he was in the pack house and safe from the storm, he could shift and they could actually spend some time together in the same space.

Lightning cracked through the air, ozone filling Vladimir's nose. He slammed the shutters closed as thunder seemed to shake the entire world. The wind picked up as he got the rest of the shutters in place and the door latched closed. Leaves swirled in the air and tree limbs swayed and shook above. Vladimir checked the cabin one more time, his heart pounding as the wind grew fiercer, the trees creaking around him. There was a loud crack followed by another as limbs fell, crashing to the ground. He raced in search of his mate, finding him and the pups pressed under the eaves at the corner of the cabin.

Vladimir scooped up all four pups. "Let's get to the pack house. Follow me." He took off along the path and around to the side of the building, past the generator, then pulled the lower-level door open. He set down the pups, and they followed Frankie inside.

Rain pelted Vladimir's back as he stepped inside and pulled the heavy door closed.

"It's all right," Vladimir said as thunder shook the building. It felt to him as though the world was angry, and this was how it came out. Maybe the goddess was upset with them, though Vladimir didn't put much stock in that kind of reasoning. The goddess provided for their needs, and they worshipped and cared for her earthly domain by hunting only for what they needed and stewarding their part of her kingdom. The pack of about forty lived within their means, made money in town selling firewood, handmade rustic furniture, and what they hunted but didn't use, and always made sure they never took too much of the goddess's bounty. Still, something was out of balance—or at least it seemed that way to him. "Are you okay?" Vladimir asked Frankie, placing a hand on his side. "It's going to be okay now. The rain has started." At least that was how things usually worked. Once the rain arrived, the worst of the wind and thunder was usually past.

That wasn't the case with this storm. The wind howled and shook the walls as rain pounded the windows. The pack gathered in the main room upstairs, with Raisa distributing tea and crackers and things to try to keep everyone calm. The room practically crackled with nervous energy as lightning lit the dark sky, followed by thunder that rattled the windows. The kids all whimpered and pressed into their parents for comfort. Frankie sat beside Vladimir, and the pups huddled near his feet as he tried not to shift his weight.

"How much longer?" little Cando, one of the children, asked quietly, his voice filled with fear. "I don't like this. Make it stop."

Vladimir's father lifted Cando into his arms. "Sometimes there are things even the alpha can't do."

Cando's eyes widened as though he couldn't believe that. Thunder cracked, and Cando buried his face in Vladimir's father's neck, holding on as his little body trembled. Vladimir knew his father was really good in situations like this. He was strong and steady, projecting an air of confidence that everyone turned to, including him.

Vladimir sat on the floor since all the chairs were taken. Frankie was so close, he was almost sitting on his lap, and Vladimir hugged him, taking comfort from his mate, with the pups piling close, their little bodies shaking.

Vladimir took some crackers and gave a few crumbs to each of the pups while still holding Frankie. It seemed strange to have a mate, but the comfort he got was surprising. He hadn't actually been able to talk to Frankie and knew next to nothing about him. That was scary in itself. What if his mate was a complete jerk when he regained his memory? Though Vladimir thought that unlikely. The goddess wouldn't do that to him, and Frankie had been taking care of a baby and four wolf cubs. Their mates were supposed to be the other half of their soul, and Vladimir knew his wasn't an asshole. That would be his brother. And as if to prove it, Dimitri strode through the pack house, kicking Vladimir's feet along the way.

"The storm is letting up and the sky is beginning to lighten," Casimir told the group, and immediately the mood began to rise. "I'm going to go check for damage."

Vladimir's father nodded his agreement, and Casimir left the room. Vladimir was afraid of what the other wolf would find. A storm like the one they'd just had was bound to make a mess.

They all got busy making food and setting it out for everyone with meat and slices of fresh bread. Vladimir let the others get what they needed and then extricated himself from the warm pile of wolves and got something for them, making sure the pups and his mate ate first. It was nice having someone to care for.

"Vladimir," his father said, having put Cando back in his mother's arms, "we're going to have to talk about what we're going to do with those pups."

He knew what his father was saying. They were going to need to learn to survive on their own.

"I know," Vladimir agreed. He turned to Frankie, who blinked back with his expressive gold eyes. Vladimir stared into them, seeing his mate looking back. Not for the first time, he wondered what Frankie looked like in his human form. Frankie's wolf was larger than his, striking, rather lanky, but fast. Vladimir translated those features to the man in his imagination.

Pulling himself out of his wandering thoughts, he looked again at Frankie, seeing his intelligent eyes tinged with fear and worry. "It will be okay."

Frankie nuzzled his hand and then laid his head on Vladimir's lap.

The storm had abated, but thunder sounded in the distance and the tension in the room rocketed upward once more. It was clear they were in for a repeat deluge as Casimir returned, wet and wrapped in a blanket. "How bad is it?"

"The cabins seem fine. There are a lot of limbs down, so we've definitely got some cleanup to do. A few trees have fallen as well. We were lucky that they missed the cabins, but the center of the compound is a mess."

Martha hurried over and rubbed his shoulders. "Come and get dressed again. It seems this isn't over yet." She returned to the baby, who so far had slept through the excitement.

The wind howled around the pack house once more, and they all settled in for a long night.

THE VARIOUS rustic rooms in the pack house were filled with families. It had been built over many years into the side of a slight hill, surrounded by the trees that grew on their land. Like most things in their lives, it was part of the land and thus a part of them. It was a meeting house as well as the living quarters of the alpha and his family, though others sometimes stayed there at the alpha's invitation. The bedroom that had been Vladimir's growing up now had Casimir, Martha, and the baby sleeping in it. The pups had whined until Martha relented and let them in as well. It seemed they wanted to be near the baby, probably to protect him.

"They're good pups," Vladimir said. He had scoped out one of the sofas, and Frankie slept near his legs, keeping them pressed to the back of the sofa. Vladimir lay awake while others in the room shuffled. He could sense the underlying fear in the room, especially when the wind grew stronger, pushing on the sides of the sturdy building, changing the air pressure, leaving dread in its wake. A few times Vladimir's sensitive ears picked up the snap and crash of tree limbs outside.

Frankie whined softly, and Vladimir soothed him gently, wishing he could make this stop and grateful that Frankie, the pups, and the baby weren't still in that cave through all of this. He closed his eyes, reaching down to his mate, wondering if he was ever going to get to look into his mate's eyes and feel his hands on him.

It was wonderful to have a mate. A lot of wolves never found theirs. Raisa always told him that for every wolf, the goddess had designed a mate. But it was up to each wolf to make the right choices in life that would allow them to meet theirs. She also reminded them often that the goddess was always with them, staying close, looking over them. Vladimir must have done something right to have met Frankie in the first place, but he couldn't help but wonder if he'd also done something wrong. Because what kind of life would he have with a mate who couldn't shift?

IT RAINED all the following morning and well into the afternoon. The wind had passed, and the pack spent the few times the rain stopped clearing the compound of debris and repairing the damaged cabins. Vladimir helped Casimir patch a hole in one of the roofs just before the clouds opened again. Fortunately his own cabin seemed to have weathered the storm without much damage.

Then, just before sunset, the rain finally stopped and the sun broke through the clouds. Vladimir had finished his chores, so he shifted to his wolf and followed his nose to Frankie. Then he took off into the woods with his mate right after him. It was time to play, to be together in the woods that sheltered and provided for them, to spend some time together as mates in the only form available to them.

Vladimir knew each tree and path, leading Frankie on a chase. He was faster and got ahead, taking Frankie deeper into the trees. Then he hid, only to pounce at

Frankie as he passed, sending them both reeling across the leafy ground. It was nice to play with his mate, running, chasing, and just being carefree for a while. It was only the two of them, and for the time being, Frankie was all his.

As the sun got lower, Vladimir led Frankie back toward the compound and to his cabin, where he shifted. Then he went inside to put out some food and water for Frankie. He ate as well—shifting took a lot of energy. Once he was dressed, he went in search of the pups and found them playing with Cando and his friends. They were having a ball, and all four wolf pups bounded over to him.

"I need to take them home, but you all can play tomorrow," Vladimir told Cando. "In fact, would you mind watching them tomorrow morning? I'm going hunting, and they need a big wolf like you to see to it that they're safe."

"I will," Cando answered, standing taller. "I watch them really good." He bent down to play some more, and Vladimir watched them for a few minutes, then said good night to Cando, gathered up the pups, and took them back to his cabin.

Night slipped quietly over the compound. For the most part, wolves embraced the darkness, so the compound had few exterior lights. Most everyone had worked hard to get the compound in order, so they quickly returned to their cabins, and the night grew nearly silent, except for the bugs sounding off and small animals scurrying through the leaves. Part of him wanted to go hunting, tracking down the little creatures, but he was tired and his belly was already full, so he returned to the cabin with Frankie and the pups, all of them curling up to sleep on his small bed.

Vladimir should have been warm and content, but he kept thinking about what he and Ruck were going to do tomorrow, what he might find... and whether it was connected to his mate.

CHAPTER 4

FRANKIE WATCHED as the pups bounded after Vladimir as if he had rabbits in his pockets, their heads up, tails bobbing, little legs prancing as he took them to their friend Cando. Finding the young wolf sitting on the ground, the pups climbed happily all over him. When Vladimir returned, he and Frankie hurried off into the woods from the back of the cabin, in the direction of the creek. Frankie loved the woods; all the smells and the sounds delighted his senses. But what he liked most was Vladimir. He liked looking at him and loved his smell. Frankie figured he could pick out that smell from a mile away if he had to. He only wished he'd he could talk to Vladimir and curl up next to him, man to man, when they were in bed.

Now that they had spent some time together, his wolf craved his mate with an all-consuming hunger that rarely left his head. His wolf wanted his mate and was getting impatient about just taking him. But Frankie wasn't keen on having sex in his wolf form—he wanted to be human when he and Vladimir came together—so the times Vladimir changed to a wolf were particularly frustrating. Frankie's wolf wanted what he wanted, and didn't understand why Frankie was holding him back.

The scent of water reached his nose, and Frankie hurried forward. He reached the stream before Vladimir, jumped into the water, and then climbed out, shaking heartily to get the water off his coat, feeling clean and washing some of his scent off. He thought about rolling in the dirt to mask more of his scent, but Ruck approached, and Frankie went on alert. He knew Ruck was Vladimir's friend, but he wasn't a wolf, and Frankie needed to protect his mate. That was part of his job, just like it was Vladimir's job to protect him.

"It's okay, buddy. I'm not going to hurt Vladimir. You can relax." Ruck stayed away until Vladimir appeared, and he approached and hugged him. Frankie still growled—he didn't like anyone touching his mate but him.

"It's okay. Ruck is my friend." Vladimir backed away, and Frankie sat down in a huff. "You're my mate, and nothing is going to change that." Vladimir knelt down, looking him in the eyes.

"Is he still not able to shift?" Ruck asked.

"No. And I'm worried. He should have been able to by now. I keep wondering if he'll ever be able to shift again." The sadness in Vladimir's voice pulled at Frankie's heart. He had tried again that morning as soon as he woke up, but nothing seemed to work. His human was there, but Frankie couldn't reach him.

"What will you do if that happens?" Ruck asked.

"He's my mate—the only one I'm ever going to get. He and I will spend our time together and figure things out."

The thought of being a wolf all the time almost broke Frankie. There were stories about shifters who went wolf. Over time they lost touch with their humanity, and the wolf took over until there was nothing else left. When that happened, they had effectively returned to their basic animal. Which meant that eventually, unless he could shift, he would forget about Vladimir, his life, and everything else. On top of that, Vladimir would have spent his life with half a mate and half his soul. Somehow he had to figure out a way to get the rest of himself back.

"Let's get going," Ruck said, and Vladimir nodded.

Frankie followed behind the others, a lot of his joy at being outside now gone. Maybe it would be best if he simply went his own way. He and Vladimir hadn't completed their bond, and over time, the attraction would fade and Vladimir would be able to find someone who could make him happy. Someone complete, who would be able to treat Vladimir the way the gentle man deserved, rather than being stuck... possibly forever.

"Can you feel it?" Vladimir asked as they crossed some sort of boundary.

The air seemed dense and still. Frankie could definitely feel that something was different, but *why*, he had no idea. The hair on his back stood up, and each step became harder. Frankie scented the air but came up with nothing out of the ordinary.

He did notice, however, that there were no small animals around. They were always present in the woods, skittering through the leaves, digging their holes, gathering food. But right now the forest was silent, which meant something was very wrong. He took each step carefully, scanning the area around him. The lack of scent and sound was almost more frightening than an actual enemy.

Still, Frankie had no illusions. He knew the enemy was out there, unseen for now, maybe hiding behind a tree or rock. His wolf continued scenting until a buzzing reached his ears. He wanted to point his head toward the sky and howl, do anything to stop the annoying sound. Then, as if his wish had been granted, it stopped.

Ruck pointed, and they went in that direction, making their way through the thick underbrush. Frankie went first, and soon Vladimir and Ruck were with him in their animal skins, using the underbrush as cover. Vladimir was a handsome wolf, and Frankie couldn't help but stop to rub against him. Ruck was nice-looking for a bear, Frankie guessed, but he only had eyes for his mate.

Ruck snorted, and Frankie pulled back. Now wasn't the time for this, but it was hard for him to not admire his mate.

All three of them came to a stop at the same time. The buzzing was back, only louder. Frankie's sensitive ears hurt. He wanted to howl, and the others seemed to be hurting as badly as he was. Then, as quickly as it started, the noise stopped again.

Frankie wanted to turn back, but he and Vladimir continued forward, stepping cautiously toward a small rise ahead of them. Vladimir crouched low, moving slowly. There wasn't a great deal of cover, just tall grasses and some scrub bushes, but it was enough for him and Vladimir. Ruck stayed at the base of the hill— his body was too big not to be seen.

Slowly, Frankie and Vladimir climbed, their bellies scraping the ground until they crested the top. The trees had been cut down, and it looked as if the land had been cleared some time ago. There were a few collapsing buildings with old stone foundations. Frankie scented carefully, but he didn't smell anything other than trees and decay, the wood from the buildings rotten and filled with moisture. He didn't see anyone and doubted anyone other than animals had been here in a long time. The old farmhouse looked like it hadn't been occupied in in decades. Frankie huffed and turned to Vladimir, who went back down the rise to where Ruck waited. Then Ruck headed off toward the north and east, around the edge of the old farm, avoiding the open area.

Maybe this was a fool's errand, though Frankie had been attacked by someone out this way. He wished he could remember something, *anything*, that might help. Not that he could explain what he knew even if he did. Not being able to shift really cut off avenues of communication.

Vladimir continued forward cautiously until they had circled the old farm. Voices reached Frankie's ears, still a distance off, but they were there on the wind. The others also stopped, probably hearing them as well. Frankie couldn't make out what the men were saying, but their scent told him they were human, as well as wolves like them. This was bad, *really* bad. If wolves were working with humans, then maybe the men knew about their pack. Frankie's heart raced and his head ached. He stopped and hid behind a tree, closing his eyes and falling to the ground, shaking.

Suddenly Vladimir was there, hands on his side. Frankie cracked his eyes open, catching a glimpse of a naked Vladimir next to him in human form. "Ruck, we need to go back."

Ruck was there was well, equally naked, covered with a forest of red hair. "We have to find out what's going on."

"He's in pain. Somehow whatever they're doing is hurting him." Vladimir seemed distressed. He lightly stroked Frankie's side, trying to comfort him.

The pressure on Frankie's head began to lessen, and he relaxed onto the forest floor, breathing heavily. The others didn't seem bothered by whatever had suddenly affected him. It had to be something about him, something wrong. Vladimir pulled his hand away, and the pressure returned in an instant. Vladimir touched him once again, and the pressure eased and then finally broke. His head cleared. Frankie breathed deeply, afraid to move. Vladimir stayed where he was, his hand still at Frankie's side, fingers burrowed into his fur.

"I don't know what to do," Vladimir whispered.

"It must be a mate thing. You can calm him. But I don't know why he's the only one affected." Ruck backed away. "I'm going to see what I can find out."

Vladimir pulled away and the pain kept its distance. Frankie continued breathing deeply, his energy sapped, so he remained still. Vladimir leaned close to him. Frankie lifted his head to rub against Vladimir's; then he motioned his head forward.

"You want me to go with him?" Vladimir asked, and Frankie whined softly, laying his head down once more. "I should find out what's going on?" Once again Frankie nodded as best he could. His only chance of moving on with his life was to know what was happening to him. Frankie was convinced it had something to do with what was going on out there. "Are you sure?"

Frankie laid his head back in the ground, closing his eyes. He wasn't sure of anything. Maybe it would be best to stay away from here. But he needed to know what had happened to him, and if the pack was at risk, then he needed to help them. They had taken him in, welcomed him into their family.

Frankie wished he could remember what had happened to his own pack. Hell, the block on his memories was just as frustrating as his inability to shift.

"We won't be gone long," Vladimir whispered. "Ruck and I will see what we can find out. Then we'll come back as quickly as we can." He patted Frankie's side lightly. "Stay hidden."

Frankie rubbed his head against Vladimir's leg, then pulled away. He missed the touch immediately, cracking his eyes open in time to see the other two shift back to their animal forms. Vladimir rubbed his head against Frankie's, and then he and Ruck hurried away.

Frankie closed his eyes once again, breathing deeply, instantly missing Vladimir. But they needed to know what was happening, and Frankie would only slow them down. He felt useless. Trapped in his wolf form, he wasn't much good to anyone. He couldn't help with the work that needed to be done, and he couldn't remember anything. If he could, they'd likely already know what was going on and would be formulating a plan to protect everyone. Instead, they were running around blind. Worse, Frankie had put his mate and Ruck in jeopardy. He had to do something.

Helpless. Frankie was helpless… and damned scared. This was why he wasn't a leader. He was content to let others make the decisions. Vladimir's idea had been solid, but now Frankie was hunched behind a tree, hoping like hell that whatever had sent him to the ground with a head that felt like it was going to explode didn't happen again. And he hated it.

He was able to get up and crouch behind the tree. His wolf wanted to go after his mate, but that would be a mistake now. They were too far away, and Frankie wouldn't be able to catch up. What if he led whoever was behind all of this right to them? No, he had to stay here; it was the right thing to do.

Frankie found a nearby thicket of branches and undergrowth and shimmied inside where he wouldn't be seen. He could barely see out between the leaves that surrounded him. He'd be safe here as long as no one got close enough to smell him. Now all he could do was wait for the others to return.

Slowly, strength returned to him. His heart beat more normally and his panting grew slower. He closed his mouth and listened, waiting for any sort of sign that the others were coming back. He hoped they wouldn't be gone too long, but then he had no idea how far they had to go. The sounds of the forest began to return. A squirrel leaped from limb to limb above him. He wanted so badly to go after it, but he stayed where he was, his wolf intent on his mate's return. Little else occupied his thoughts.

A twig broke off to the side, and Frankie crouched lower.

"I saw something move in this direction."

Frankie raised his nose and scented. Humans.

"I don't know what it was, but there were two of them."

"Probably animals," another voice said. Both were men, and they stank like they hadn't bathed in quite a while. Sweat, piss, even bad cologne that irritated

Frankie's nose, all mixed into an obnoxious cocktail. "I don't see anything at all, and I want to get back."

"We were told to watch the perimeter in case there was anyone out here, so that's what we'll do," the first voice snapped. A twig broke close to where Frankie was hiding. "Over there. Look. What the hell is that?"

"A bear," the other man said. "I don't like this, Hank. No one said there were bears out here. A little gold ain't worth getting ripped to shreds for."

"Just fucking shoot it, Greg," the one called Hank said.

"These rifles aren't strong enough. Even if we hit it, the shot will only make it angry. That thing could rip us apart before we got away. Just stay still. It's going away," Greg whispered, the scent of fear, acrid and sharp, filling the air. Frankie willed Ruck to stay away from the men.

"A wolf," Hank whispered. "There aren't any wolves in Pennsylvania. At least there haven't been for a hundred years." He stepped close enough that Frankie could see his scrubby boots.

"You're seeing things. Must be a mountain lion or something," Greg dismissed, but Frankie didn't feel any more at ease. It didn't matter if they thought Vladimir was a mountain lion or a wolf. If they shot him, they could kill his mate. "I think they're gone." A growl reached his ears, and the fear washing off the two men grew exponentially. "I'm getting out of here."

"Stay right there. I'll shoot anything that comes close," Hank boasted, backing so close to the thicket that his boots nearly touched Frankie.

He had to do something.

He was seconds away from attacking when his mind clouded and his human half burst forth. Without thinking, Frankie began to change, even as he leapt from the thicket. By the time his feet hit the ground, he was on two legs, grasping one of the men by the throat, throwing him into the other one with all the force he had. A gun discharged, but Frankie didn't stop, holding the two men down while Vladimir and Ruck raced up, now also in human form.

"What the fuck are you doing out here naked?" Greg demanded just before Frankie clobbered him on the side of the head with a log. He went down. Hank turned to attack, but Frankie swung the log again, knocking him out as well.

"Frankie?" Vladimir asked, standing next to him, with Ruck racing up as well. "What happened?"

"They were going to shoot you," he answered breathily. "We need to get out of here."

Ruck checked both men. "They're out, but breathing," he declared and then took off into the woods.

"Come on. Let's leave them for their friends to find. We need to get away before we're seen. I can tell you what we found when we get back." Vladimir took Frankie's hand, tugging him in the direction Ruck had gone. Once they were out of sight of the humans, Ruck shifted back to his bear.

"I don't know if I can," Frankie said. "What if I can't shift back again?"

"I bet you can. You have contact with both halves of yourself now. And we need to get away from here fast in case they come after us." Vladimir looked him over from head to toe, smiling. "Besides, I don't want those assholes looking at you." He growled, and Frankie thought of his wolf, his bones repositioning until he stood on all fours once again. Vladimir followed him, and then they raced off into the trees, Frankie following Vladimir as fast as they could possibly go.

It felt great to run like this with his mate again. He tried to put the reason for the haste out of his mind, keeping a close eye on Vladimir. He had finally been able to shift, and even as he ran, he could feel his human half near the surface once again. He was relieved. Maybe tonight when the two of them were alone, they could finally become the kind of mates Frankie had always hoped for.

WHEN THEY reached the stream, Ruck shifted back and pulled on his clothes. Vladimir did the same, but Frankie stayed in his wolf form. Most wolves didn't bother about nudity. It was just a part of life. But Frankie wasn't keen on walking back into the compound naked. "I'll have some clothes for you when we get to the cabin," Vladimir said.

Frankie rubbed against his mate and followed him back to the small cabin, where he shifted back to human. "God, I was beginning to wonder if I would ever be able to do that again." He accepted the light pants and T-shirt from Vladimir. "Thank you." His gaze went down to his feet. He wriggled his toes, wishing he had shoes. Anything Vladimir had would be too small for Frankie's feet.

"I'll see if anyone has any shoes that will fit you." Then Vladimir left the cabin and returned a few minutes later with a worn pair of sneakers. "Casimir had these." Fortunately they were close to the right size.

"I have a ton of questions," Frankie said.

"So do we. Do you know where you came from?"

Frankie shook his head. "I don't remember much. I know I used to have a pack, and Victor was part of that. I know something bad happened, but I can't remember what it was or how I came to be in that cave. I remember some stuff after that, like taking care of Victor for about two weeks. I found the pups and didn't want them to die. But there are huge gaps in my memory."

"Okay." Vladimir sat on the edge of the bed and patted the mattress. Frankie sat next to him. "Do you remember who attacked you?"

Frankie shook his head. "All I remember was that it wasn't a wolf. And then there was a sharp pain in my back, burning…. Then that was it."

"So you don't think the silver knife had anything to do with your memory loss?" Vladimir took his hand.

"I don't think so. I could shift before I was attacked. That was how I got food for myself and the pups. I hunted and brought it back." His head was still fuzzy. "I wish I could help you."

"Do you remember where your old pack was?"

"In southern New York, I think." He paused. "Yeah, it was. My uncle was alpha and my aunt the grand dame. I know what happened to them, but it seems lost now. I know I ended up alone and well away from the pack with Victor. I can only assume that something happened to the pack and I had to take off with Victor to keep him safe. Other than that, most of my life is a complete mystery. I know who I am… sort of… but much of what makes me the person I am is sort of lost in the ether of my memory."

"You don't remember your childhood? What about your parents?"

"That I remember. My mom and dad were part of my uncle's pack. Dad was a beta wolf, and he always stood beside my uncle." Frankie huffed and sat quietly. "I stayed with that pack for most of my life until my uncle was challenged for leadership, and then... all I remember is living in the cave."

"Not how you got there?" Vladimir asked. Frankie shook his head. "You're a long way from your pack lands."

"I know. My feet hurt, so I think I walked a long way." It was troubling not to be able to remember anything. "I knew your pack was here but wasn't sure if they would welcome us, so I made sure I stayed off your land." He tried to remember the reasons he'd done what he had, but came up empty. "I think I was out hunting when I was attacked. I know I was trying to lead someone away from the cave to protect Victor and the pups. After I was hurt, I tried to get back to them. They needed me. That's the last thing I remember." Frankie squeezed Vladimir's hand. "Then I woke up and you were there. My head was messed up and you were carrying me." He knew he sounded completely crazy. He hoped Vladimir believed him.

Vladimir shook his head. "I've never heard of someone getting amnesia from silver poisoning. Maybe we can ask Raisa what else could cause that kind of loss. There has to be something. Trauma, maybe? No one just forgets everything about themselves for no reason."

This was getting depressing. It was time to change the subject. "What did you find in the woods?" Frankie asked. "The people I fought were humans. They didn't smell like wolves at all."

"Yeah. We found a group of humans, though I think there were some wolves there too. It was hard to tell with all the overlapping smells. I don't know if the humans were aware of the wolves or not, but they were in this big camp with lots of equipment and what looked like water raceways. It smelled bad, and Ruck said he felt sick. They didn't see us, and we were able to watch them for a while without being noticed."

"Is all this about mining?" Frankie asked, half to himself. "If that's true, they could be hurting the water." He tried to think of how the stream flowed and realized that the humans were downstream. At least the pack wasn't going to get sick.

"The stream weaves all through the forest. That could be the darkness that's spreading. Maybe there's something in the water that's poisoning the forest. I'm not sure, but those men are dangerous. I could smell them well into our territory. They could come across the pack any time. And if they're destroying the stream, then the forest is going to be next."

A knock sounded and then the door opened and Vladimir's father charged inside in full alpha mode. "I see you were able to shift."

Frankie nodded under his steely gaze. "Vladimir was in danger, and I shifted right there." He wasn't sure how much he should say about where they had been, so he kept quiet.

The alpha turned to Vladimir. "I understand that you and your mate here decided to go off on your own to see what you could find out." His lips formed a straight line. "Why do you have to disobey me all the time?"

Vladimir seemed stunned for a second, tilting his head to the side in confusion that Frankie could almost feel himself. Frankie knew Vladimir hadn't expected his father to accept him in a relationship with another man, and yet it seemed to have just happened. Frankie was a little confused and incredibly grateful. "We need to know what the threats are," Vladimir answered, still confused even as the tension in his body lessened.

"I'm well aware of those men and where they are. That's why I declared that part of our territory off-limits." He stalked closer.

"Then what are we going to do about it?" Vladimir asked, lowering his gaze. The alpha didn't seem to have an answer. That surprised Frankie. Vladimir's father remained quiet and surprisingly calm. Frankie had expected a show of force to back up his position. That was how wolf society usually worked—disobedience was brought to heel. "We have to do something," Vladimir said.

"I was going to," the alpha answered. "But Frankie here and his silver knife changed everything. I could get the pack together and overrun them, scare the lot of them off. Except how many would be hurt? Then what would happen? The humans would return with more and hunt us all down. To make matters worse, the silver knife means that someone knows about us. Is it one of them? I don't know."

"There were shifters in the camp, Father," Vladimir told him. "At least two or three. We could scent them. They must be acting like the humans, because the men said something about there not being wolves in Pennsylvania. So they mustn't know. But they *are* working together. And that's a problem for all of us." He hung his head. "Still, I'm sorry I disobeyed you."

The alpha pulled out a chair and sat rigidly. "No, you're not. That's the problem. You do whatever you want and act contrite when you get back… then you do it again." The alpha leaned closer. "This can't continue. It hurts the entire pack. They want order and need to know what to expect. You're becoming a challenge to that order, so it must stop. You need to ask permission before you hunt or leave the compound. You must tell me where you are and what you're doing. No more sneaking off. You could have been hurt—all of you, including the bear." His glare was harsh. It left Frankie feeling cold.

"I apologize, Alpha," Frankie said quietly, hanging his head, his belly fluttering in a bad way.

"I understand, Father," Vladimir said. "I was only trying to help."

The alpha nodded. "I know you were. But if you bring those men down on the entire pack, what will we do? Being alpha means that I have to think of the entire pack. I'm responsible for the safety and well-being of everyone, and the decisions I make are for everyone's benefit. Not my own."

"I'm sorry, Father," Vladimir repeated, baring his neck to his dad. It was a humbling experience, and Frankie did the same thing. He felt terrible that he had gone against the alpha's wishes. Frankie wasn't even a member of the pack yet and he was already causing trouble. "But grateful too… for Frankie and your acceptance." Vladimir swallowed, and damned if a touch of humility didn't look good on him.

The alpha sat quietly for a few seconds. "Tell me what you saw." It seemed to be easier to talk about the situation at hand than the two of them.

Vladimir lifted his gaze from his shoes, and Frankie did the same.

"We think they're mining the stream for gold. They have pumps and water running into a large building and out again, and it smells really bad, like chemicals. It burned my nose and made Ruck feel sick. They have engines that whistle, and something in the air gave Frankie a massive headache. He stayed behind while Ruck and I got closer. Like I said, we could smell wolves there too."

"Wait," Frankie interrupted. "They don't know about us. At least, not all of them do." He faced the alpha. "When I couldn't go on, I hid." He figured justifying what he'd done was out of the question, so he just relayed what he'd heard. "The thing is, they saw Ruck and Vladimir in their animal forms. They thought they were just animals."

The alpha leaned forward. "They saw a wolf. And there are almost no wolves left in this area."

"That isn't correct, as we know from the pups. But you're right. They convinced themselves that Vladimir was really a mountain lion. But still, they just thought he and Ruck were animals. There was no mention of shifters. Which is good." Even as Frankie said the words, the full weight of what they'd done settled on him. Frankie had hurt both of those men. It was possible that they were going to come looking for the person who'd attacked them. And that could lead them to the pack.

The alpha rubbed the back of his neck. "We bought this land many years ago and have lived here since, building our homes and making a living off what the goddess provides. The pack survives here because we keep to ourselves. The valley we're in is small and wooded, providing us with plenty of cover. The old farm is growing over more and more each year. But now these men know there's something out here. They may investigate, and what will we do if they find us?" He stood. "I forbid either of you to leave the compound. We are all going to need to stay close. We can't expose ourselves to anyone." He glared at both of them. "Vladimir, I had hoped that meeting your mate would make you more cautious. Instead you endangered your mate's life because you were curious, and now you might have risked exposure of us all." He turned and left the cabin, pulling the door closed behind him.

Vladimir didn't move, and Frankie slid closer to try to comfort his mate. "I'm sorry about all this."

"It's not your fault," Vladimir said. "And one good thing came out of it. You're able to shift." He smiled wanly. "That's great, but why would you want a mate like me? I just lead everyone into trouble. Dad is angry with me, and both you and Ruck could have been hurt because I had to find out what was happening." Through their bond, Frankie felt the hurt that welled inside Vladimir. It wasn't as sharp as his own pain, but it was there. He could feel the pain in his chest like an ache.

"Did your pack ever talk about what it means to have a mate?" Frankie asked.

Vladimir nodded. "Did yours?"

"I think so." He concentrated, tugging at the edges of the blank areas of his mind, trying to make a connection with what he knew was there. "We don't get to choose our mates, and we only get one." Frankie swallowed hard. "I remember. I can remember… something. My father took me aside and told me that our mates are the other half of ourselves and that the goddess gifts that person to us. But we have to be lucky enough to find them. Then he said that people like me don't get mates." His heart ached, and he turned away. Vladimir held his hand more tightly. "My dad found out that I was gay, and he was terrible about it. I remember him yelling at me, and then, when he calmed down, he told me that as long as I stayed on that path, I would never have a mate… that I should turn away from the way I am and find a real mate. He thought I should find one of the females in the pack… mate with her… and go on with my life." Frankie sighed. What a terrible thing to remember. He would have been better off if that memory had remained forgotten.

"He wanted you to marry someone you didn't love?" Vladimir asked.

Frankie nodded. "I remember playing with Marly when I was small. I think we'd known each other all our lives, and Dad wanted us to mate and have pups. Lots of pups." He was trying to piece together his memory with just brief snippets of recollection as glue. "Why would you want half a person as a mate? I don't really know who I am, but my own father, it seemed, didn't want me for who I was. Why should you or anyone?"

He wasn't sure what kind of reaction he expected, but Vladimir hugging him, holding him tightly, and then kissing him was so far out of his expectations that he sat still in shock before hugging Vladimir back. In those few seconds, a sense of deep peace washed over him, followed by deep-seated desire. Frankie pulled back as that desire threatened to overwhelm him. He breathed deeply and stood up, moving away from Vladimir.

"What is it? Did I do something wrong?"

Frankie shook his head. "I don't know who I am." He paced the floor of the cabin, his wolf pressing to get out and jump Vladimir. His wolf knew what it wanted, but Frankie was hesitant. "I just remembered that stuff about my father, and I know there's more, but I don't know what it is. What if I'm a complete asshole and I stole Victor or something?" His gut told him that wasn't true, but Frankie wasn't sure what to believe. He wished he had some answers.

Vladimir stood and placed his arms around Frankie, and a calm instantly replaced the agitation that threatened to overtake him. "Frankie, I doubt that is true. If it was, you wouldn't be so worried about it. Our memories are a big part of who we are… but they don't make up the whole person. And even if you can't remember, you still know right from wrong."

"Do I?"

Vladimir held him tighter. "I think so. You aren't like my brother, Dimitri. He's my father's heir, and Dad thinks the sun rises and sets on his wolfy butt. But Dimitri isn't a good guy. Sure, he goes out hunting for days and usually brings home a deer for the pack. But that's not all he does. He goes out in the human world, screwing anything that moves. I can smell it on him sometimes. He's been more careful lately about how he smells when he gets home, but I know how he acts. Whatever he wants, Dimitri feels no compunction about taking. That isn't you. I know that." Vladimir rested his head on Frankie's shoulder. "The goddess would never give me a mate like that. She wouldn't be that cruel. Sometimes I don't understand the goddess at all, the way she allows bad things to happen, but I know she's not cruel."

"I don't know much of anything." Frankie closed his eyes and held Vladimir in return.

"What does your heart say?" Vladimir asked.

Frankie had to admit that his heart was already set on Vladimir. His wolf paced, tail wagging, excited and ready to pounce. His gut told him that his wolf wouldn't steer him wrong. Frankie's wolf represented the instinctual side of his personality, and his instincts had never led him astray. How he knew that for a fact wasn't clear, but his gut told him emphatically that was true.

A bang on the door had both of them jumping apart. "Vladimir...."

Suddenly the door swung open hard. "Come get these wolf pups before I take them down to the stream and drown them. They're getting into everything and won't leave me the hell alone." Dimitri had two of the pups in his arms while the others nipped at his feet, growling and jumping back and forth, their tails still, teeth bared. Damn, what sort of person managed to piss the playful wolf cubs off?

Frankie took the pissed-off pups from Dimitri— one of them trying to bite Dimitri's hand as he did— while Vladimir snagged the others off the floor. "Come on. They're just pups."

Dimitri whirled around and slammed the door on his way out.

Frankie shook his head. "I see what you mean. If pups don't like him...."

"Yeah." Vladimir soothed the two rambunctious bundles of fur before putting them down on the floor with the others. They immediately began chasing one another as Vladimir got them some food and water. Then they attacked their dish, jostling until the food was gone. The four of them settled on the blanket at the foot of the bed and curled together to sleep. "How can anyone not love them?"

"Maybe the pups have more sense than most of us," Frankie offered.

"We should go see what there is to eat ourselves, before the others devour it." Vladimir opened the door, and they hurried outside before the pups could follow them, then headed to the pack house.

CHAPTER 5

VLADIMIR SAT at the large table with Frankie next to him, their thighs touching under the table. "I need to speak to your father after dinner. Is that possible?" Frankie asked Vladimir.

The alpha, who'd obviously heard him, made eye contact and nodded. Vladimir figured Frankie didn't want to keep taking the pack's hospitality without making a contribution to everyone's well-being.

He ate, listening to the others chat about what was going on in their lives. It seemed another cabin was to be built, this one for Dimitri and his eventual mate. Vladimir had heard rumors, but this was the first time detailed plans were being discussed.

"Does he have a mate?" Frankie asked.

Vladimir shook his head. As far as he knew, Dimitri was a free agent, screwing anyone he could get his paws on.

"This is Father's way of pushing him to go out, find a mate, and return to lead the pack," Vladimir explained.

Dimitri must have heard him, and he bared his teeth from across the table, letting Vladimir know he didn't appreciate being talked about. Not that

Vladimir cared. Dimitri was nothing but a bully, getting whatever he wanted by pushing everyone else around. Vladimir doubted Dimitri had any intention of finding his mate. He was having too good a time playing the field. Still, if he got a human woman pregnant, there would be trouble. But that would be Dimitri's and his father's problem, thank the goddess.

"I heard that bears are invading our territory," Dimitri said. "Maybe I should go out hunting and take care of the problem."

"Maybe you should mind your own business and do more to earn your place in the pack," the alpha said.

Vladimir hid his smile at the rebuke from their dad. It was rare that the alpha got after Dimitri for anything.

"You need to settle down. As for bears near our pack lands, as long as they keep to themselves, we'll do the same. There is no need to antagonize any of our neighbors." He returned to his dinner as Martha sat down next to Frankie with Victor sleeping in her arms. She gently passed him to Frankie to hold while she ate her dinner.

"He's a wonderful baby. Happy, content, and always hungry." She smiled brightly.

Frankie let Victor hold his finger while he slept. "I wish I could remember how he came to me." He watched Victor even as his expression grew sadder. "I can't remember much about my life." The table grew largely quiet as Frankie talked. "I spent weeks in that cave, scared and wondering if any of us were going to survive. Thank the goddess that wolf babies are strong. I was scared every day that Victor would get sick or that I would run out of what I needed for him. I thought of coming here and throwing myself on your pack's mercy, but I was afraid—for myself and for him. I'm not sure if I was thinking clearly. Everything seemed turned around."

"As if you had nothing to draw from?" Raisa asked from her seat down the table. Frankie nodded. "And everything that you could use as a guidepost in your life had been stripped away?"

"Exactly," Frankie said softly.

"That sounds like some sort of poisoning. But not silver. That would be harsher and more direct." She glanced around at the others. "Let me do some thinking about it." She returned to her dinner, and Frankie settled back in his seat, humming to little Victor.

"Do you want him to stay with you now?" Martha asked, almost painfully.

Frankie smiled at Martha. "He's going to be better off with you." He rocked Victor slowly. "I have vague recollections of him in my memory, and I know he isn't my child. I would never let him want for anything, but...." He returned his attention to Martha. "Your expression tells me that Victor has already found a place in your heart."

Martha nodded, and Casimir took her hand and whispered very softly into her ear. She leaned against him. It was the closest to tears that Vladimir had ever seen her.

"He has...," Martha whispered hoarsely. Vladimir knew that Martha and Casimir wanted a child more than anything in the world, and Frankie's generosity and unselfishness touched his heart. It was clear that Frankie cared for Victor, but it was also pretty obvious that Martha and Casimir already loved the child.

He was pretty sure that Frankie understood that, as well.

CHAPTER 6

"HE SHOULD stay with you," Frankie said.

The expression on Martha's face nearly broke Frankie's heart. It was clear that she already adored Victor, and the child deserved that kind of love. Not that Frankie didn't care for the little boy. He was a joy. But this was a pack, and Victor would need that. In a pack, everyone helped raise and care for young wolves. Cubs brought the pack together and gave it life. So it wouldn't be like Frankie was giving him up. He was doing what he thought was best for the baby. "He definitely seems happy."

"Martha and I adore the little guy," Casimir said, the big beta wolf's voice breaking a little. Frankie had come to understand feeling loss and longing over the past few weeks, even if he couldn't fully remember why it was still there, and he saw it reflected back at him from both of them. A child wasn't something to be bartered or passed around, and Frankie knew that these two would cherish Victor. That was the most important thing.

The alpha finished eating and left the table, with Dimitri walking right behind him. They went into the office, and Dimitri closed the door. Frankie figured he'd wait until they were done before trying to speak to Vladimir's father.

Vladimir had other ideas, though. Once they were finished, they took care of their dishes, and Frankie thanked everyone for a wonderful meal. Then Vladimir walked over to his father's office and knocked on the door.

He motioned Frankie over, and when his father called out for them to enter, he opened the door and they went inside together.

Dimitri turned as soon as Frankie walked in, his features stormy, anger radiating off him. He stood and stomped out of the office, slamming the door hard enough to make Frankie jump at the sharp sound.

"What's that about, Dad?"

The alpha leaned forward. "Your brother doesn't think we should trust Frankie here. He thinks he's going to ask to join the pack."

"He is my mate, Dad," Vladimir said, and the alpha nodded. Power washed over him, and Frankie got a pretty good idea that Dimitri's show of temper wasn't going to do him any good. That was a relief. "Why wouldn't he petition to join us? Unless you want me to leave."

Alpha Corelia shook his head. "I don't. And I've been expecting Frankie to petition to join us. Still, now that he's able to shift, I want Frankie to explain some things to me." He sat rigidly in his chair, and both Frankie and Vladimir did the same.

"I'll tell you anything I can. But there are large portions of my memory that seem closed to me." The longer his memory remained clouded, the more he feared it might never return. "That's the best way I can describe it." Vladimir took his hand, threading their fingers together. "But I know I want to be with Vladimir, and I want to contribute to the pack. You've all been kind to me these past few days, and I want to help."

"What skills do you have?" the alpha asked.

Frankie shrugged. "I can build and am good with my hands. At least I think I am. I have snippets of memories of helping to build cabins at my former pack." He stilled. "I should tell you that I also have other flashes of memory—of my father telling me that my kind, like Vladimir's, don't get mates. He was very angry with me. I'll understand if…."

The alpha smiled. "While I don't understand two males mating, I can tell from here that you are mates, and if the goddess wills it, I'm not going to second-guess her wisdom. As for what you remember, Raisa has spoken to me about it. While she isn't sure of the cause, she feels that your memory loss is real and that it isn't something you can control."

"Dad," Vladimir interjected.

"It's okay," Frankie said. "He's doing what's best for the pack. I wouldn't expect a good alpha to do anything less. He needs to make sure I'm not a threat to anyone else. And I wish I could give him that assurance. But I can't. I was attacked and someone stabbed me with a silver knife. So another wolf, or someone who knows about wolves, wants me dead." He swallowed hard. "I don't know why, or where that person came from." He began to shake. "If it had been a direct challenge… at least I would be able to see the face of the person. But…."

"Silver knives and poisoning are for the low and unsavory. It was the work of a coward," Alpha Corelia spat. "And that you survived tells me that you're a strong wolf. There aren't many who would have been able to recover." He watched both of them. "I'll welcome you as a member of the pack at the next full moon. I want you to see Casimir. He'll help you find a work detail. We're planning an additional cabin." He raised his voice. "It was supposed to be for Dimitri, but if he doesn't stop the carousing he thinks I don't know about, we'll use it for someone else, maybe a growing family." He smiled, probably knowing that Dimitri had heard what he'd said. "You can help with the planning and construction."

"I'll do my best," Frankie agreed with a smile, glancing at Vladimir. "Thank you." He stood, and they shook hands with the alpha. To Frankie's surprise, Vladimir's father came around the desk and hugged him, transferring scent. Frankie knew that as soon as he left the room, everyone would know that he had been accepted into the pack.

Frankie thanked the alpha once again, and they left the office, passing a scowling Dimitri to join the rest of the pack, who had pulled out some games and were playing around a table. "The pack tends to be vicious when it comes to these games."

"But they're playing Sorry!, the board game. How do you make that vicious?"

Vladimir pressed his lips to his ear. "See the marks on the table? Those are the losers' claw marks. The pack takes winning as a serious challenge." Vladimir guided him away from the table as the growls started and the scent of aggression built in the air. "I told you."

"But I like that game," Frankie said without really thinking. He didn't know how, but he was sure he did.

"You can play if you want. I need to check on the pups and make sure they haven't torn the cabin apart."

Frankie shook his head and followed Vladimir out of the pack house, the desire that had remained banked through dinner flaring to life again, growing hotter with each step. His wolf pranced and paced, ready to pounce. When they reached the small cabin, Vladimir carefully opened the door. Frankie half expected a mess, but the pups were asleep on their blanket. At the noise, they woke and raced to greet them excitedly. Frankie and Vladimir managed to get the door closed, and between them they fed the pups and played with them, trying to wear the little bundles of energy out. After a few hours of chasing, they finally pranced to the blanket, curled into a pile, and went to sleep.

"I thought they were going to stay up all night," Frankie said as he got cleaned up and then undressed. Vladimir's bed was quite small, and he waited to see what Vladimir expected. They hadn't talked about sleeping now that Frankie was in his human form.

Vladimir undressed, baring his golden skin to Frankie. Frankie's wolf loved what he saw, and the scent of arousal filled the air. Frankie gasped when Vladimir drew him close, their bodies pressing together. He hissed and groaned as heat mixed with erotic tension to stoke a fire that threatened to consume him.

From somewhere in his foggy memory, he remembered stories about what it was like to have a mate, but the truth was even better than the stories. It was as if they could almost read each other's mind. "Come to bed."

Frankie nodded. "I wasn't sure what you'd want to do." He had been afraid Vladimir would insist on waiting or be tentative because there was so much that

Frankie couldn't remember. But it seemed their wolves had other ideas… and they were in control now. Frankie lay down, and Vladimir practically pounced on him, making the bed springs bounce under them. "Going a little wolfy?" Frankie asked.

"I guess so," Vladimir growled and kissed him, stilling further conversation.

Frankie closed his arms around Vladimir, exploring his back and incredibly hard butt as Vladimir took possession of his lips. Lust and desire clouded Frankie's brain when Vladimir flexed his hips, causing their cocks to rub together in a dance that he knew was only the warm-up.

"I want you."

Frankie panted. "Then take me. Make me yours." Days of being close and yet unable to do anything had practically driven Frankie crazy. His mate had been right next to him, and they hadn't been able to complete the bond. It was all Frankie wanted.

It took Frankie a few seconds to realize that Vladimir had stopped. "What? Did I do something wrong?"

"No." Vladimir swallowed. "I want you, but I can't mate with you… not yet. You need to be able to make the decision freely, knowing all there is to know about yourself. Once we do this, we can't go back. I won't do that to you. Not like this." He smoothed Frankie's floppy hair out of his eyes. "It isn't that I don't want to. It's just that we both need to be sure."

"But…."

"Sweetheart, I can still make you mine. It's just that I'm not going to bite and mark you to complete the mating. Not yet." He kissed him once again, his passion obvious in every touch. "I just want you to have the chance to remember who you are. Once you do, I'll take you as mine forever."

Part of Frankie was disappointed, but he understood. Still, what if Vladimir changed his mind? The very notion sent a wave of fear through him, and in true mate style, Vladimir noticed.

"Hey, you're still my mate, and I will fight anyone who tries to hurt you." He cradled Frankie's cheek in his hand. "It's just that I think we should wait for the final step." He parted Frankie's legs, opening Frankie to him. "Do you still want me?"

"Oh goddess, yes," Frankie whispered, and Vladimir pressed himself to his opening. Frankie wasn't a virgin, but it surprised him that his body seemed to know Vladimir was his mate. There was no hesitation, no nerves… it just felt right. He opened to him, and the two of them joined together in a wave of ecstasy that sent Frankie's mind reeling.

"Did I hurt you?" Vladimir asked, and Frankie realized he'd cried out. He shook his head, tugging Vladimir down to him, kissing him hard.

"No." Vladimir moved slowly, and Frankie growled. "Don't stop."

"I don't think I could if I tried," Vladimir said as his eyes shifted. Frankie felt his do the same, plunging the world into black and white. Not that he cared—his senses only heightened. Frankie inhaled the scent of Vladimir's sweat and deep musk as they moved together. The scent only got more intense the longer they were connected.

The room was nearly dark, but his enhanced sight was enough for him to take in the roll of Vladimir's hips, his sleek chest and belly, slender hips, and long arms. His mate was handsome, glistening with a hint of sweat. "That's it, just love me."

"I already do," Vladimir whispered and kissed him hard, stealing Frankie's breath. He had no idea how Vladimir could possibly love him already, but Frankie could feel those same emotions surfacing. It made sense. They were fated mates, and in a way, their hearts had been looking for each other for most of their lives. It was so easy for Frankie to fall for Vladimir. He was just the kind of person Frankie needed. He was strong—a leader, even if he didn't know it. Vladimir was also sexy as hell, and each touch sent Frankie's desire racing for the moon.

"Vladdy," Frankie whispered as his head swam. All conscious thought seemed to take a back seat to instinct. His wolf wanted more, and he was determined to get it. Frankie rocked with Vladimir, gripping the bedding to keep from flying apart. His fingers shifted to claws and he had to pull his hands way to keep from shredding the sheets.

He had never experienced this type of intense passion before. Vladimir rolled his hips and leaned closer. Musk, sweat, and a hint of sweetness filled Frankie's nose. He could hear Vladimir's heartbeat as well as feel its pull. His spirit seemed to have a will of its own, and he went right along with it.

"Oh goddess," Frankie whimpered and clamped his eyes closed, afraid they'd pop out of his head under the amazing pressure. Never had he felt so full, so intense, so complete—both excited and right at the same time. This was something he'd never thought possible, and when he slid his eyes open, taking in his mate, his heart leapt even higher.

"Hang on, sweetheart," Vladimir whispered. "I can feel your control slipping. Keep your wolf at bay and put yourself in my hands. I will never hurt you, either part of you, if I can possibly help it."

Frankie growled deep and long, his wolf so damned near the surface, it took all his effort to keep it under control.

Frankie's entire body tingled, and from his feet, to the base of his spine, to his neck, the sensation fanned out like ripples in a pond, reinforcing itself until Frankie could hold back no longer. He held Vladimir tightly, whimpering to contain the last of his shredding control, until Vladimir kissed him hard, sending him over the edge, cock throbbing without being touched.

His release blew his mind. Frankie wondered if his entire brain had short-circuited. Vladimir's heartbeat pounded in his ears and his teeth elongated, mouth drawn to the spot at the base of his mate's neck. Vladimir pulled back as if understanding exactly what Frankie's wolf had in mind. He stilled and waited. "Just relax," Vladimir said in a deep, rich voice, and Frankie realized it was his wolf communicating to Frankie's. He had never known that to happen before. Granted, the wolf and the man were simply halves of the same person, so why wouldn't the wolf have a voice that could come through Vladimir's human half?

"I'm okay," Frankie answered with a smile of complete contentment. His eyes were already drifting closed, both halves of him completely worn out. He shivered and groaned as their bodies separated. He instantly missed the connection. And he was a mess.

Vladimir got a cloth and wiped him up before returning to the bed and climbing in next to him, cuddling tight. This reminded Frankie of when he was young with the other pups in the pack. They'd slept in a pile, curled together, their little wolves running free no matter what form they were in. Frankie felt safe and secure, his head finally settling in the here and now instead of thinking about who might want to hurt him.

CHAPTER 7

VLADIMIR WOKE to Frankie pressing against him and the pups playing on the bed, getting as close as they could. It truly was like a puppy pile, and he didn't want to move, but they had things they needed to do today, and Vladimir could hear the rest of the pack stirring and getting ready for work.

"Sweetheart," he whispered without moving. In truth, he loved having Frankie next to him and wasn't keen on breaking the intimacy.

Frankie hummed and burrowed further under the covers while the pups lifted their heads, yawned, and pounced on him, growling and ready to play.

"Guys, I'm not a chew toy," Frankie muttered, pulling his hand under the covers. Of course, that didn't stop the pups. They tried burrowing under, still growling, tails going a mile a minute.

"I'll get up and feed these four. I thought maybe this afternoon we could shift and teach them how to hunt. They're going to need to learn to be self-sufficient, and instinct won't be enough."

Frankie growled, and the pups backed away, their front paws forward, butts in the air, ready for whatever Frankie did. "Okay, I'll get up, you rascals," he groaned. He pushed down the blankets, covering the pups, who shimmied to get from under the blankets.

Vladimir got their food ready, and they raced over, jostling to eat like… well, wolves.

Frankie slid his arms around Vladimir's waist, pressing himself against his mate's warm, bare skin. "You know, I could try to entice you back to bed." Frankie's belly rumbled. "Then again… maybe after I've eaten."

"Get dressed and we'll see what's going on in the pack house. Then we can find Casimir and check out the new cabin." Vladimir had an excess of energy this morning and was ready to get going, but he turned in Frankie's arms and kissed him, drawing him close as he cupped Frankie's hot butt. God, he'd never thought about it, but he was definitely turning into as ass man, especially this particular one.

"I think I could be enticed," Frankie whispered—and then jumped at the pounding on his door.

"Come on, lovebirds, we have things we need to do. Get your butts out of bed." The humor in Casimir's voice was unmistakable.

Vladimir chuckled softly as they broke apart. "We're on our way. You might not want to come in unless you're keen to see some man-on-man action." All he got was a growl in response.

"WHAT DO you want me to do?" Frankie asked when the two of them had joined Casimir and Sasha on the other side of the compound, where he was laying out string to mark the outline of the new cabin. "Wait. That isn't straight, and the ground here isn't going to be good for a building." He took a shovel that was leaning against one of the trees and dug into the ground. "The stream once ran right through here." He made a line with his hand indicating the old stream bed. "The soil here is going to be made up of lots of dried sediment. It'll be unstable." He dug down a ways and showed Casimir the fine sand and grit underneath.

"How did you know that?" Casimir asked as Vladimir looked on in wonder.

Frankie shrugged. "I don't know. I just did. If you look carefully, the slight dip in the land is actually the path of the old stream before it changed to its present course. I suggest that we relocate the cabin over there," he said, pointing. "It's only about twenty feet or so, but the ground is much more stable." He smiled, and Casimir nodded. "Do we need to ask the alpha's permission?"

"Let's lay everything out and then bring him down to review what we have and get his blessing," Vladimir suggested. Casimir agreed, as did the other men.

Casimir went over the plans. The cabin wasn't going to be huge, only about fifteen by twenty feet—somewhat larger than the one Vladimir and Frankie were sharing, but not a mansion by any means. "We've already cut most of the trees and stripped them down. We did that when we cleared the land over here."

Vladimir couldn't help looking up at the canopy overhead. Minimal trees had been removed, to keep as much forest cover as possible. The thinning provided for pockets of sunlight for new growth and allowed parts of the forest to renew themselves.

"It's pretty simple," Casimir explained.

"Yes," Frankie agreed. "But we could do a little more. If we used two courses of logs at the top, it would create a sleeping loft above and open up the space below for living. Our cabin is heated with a stove, and I really like that. We have all that rock from the stream, so we could build a stone section in one corner for the stove. It would keep the walls from drying out as quickly. Or we could just add a chimney with a fireplace, if you want. But that's a lot more work."

"A stove should work, and we already have the stone," Vladimir said. "I gathered most of it." He motioned to the pile of even-sized rocks stacked off to the side.

"What about the floor?" Frankie asked.

"We'll plank it like yours and Vladimir's," Casimir suggested. "It's simple, but it works and it stays solid for a long time. We can also use the larger tree branches that don't work for the log walls to make the planks."

"We need to make use of everything," Vladimir added. "Sasha makes amazing furniture. He did what's in our cabin," he said to Frankie, nodding toward the man who was walking closer to them. Vladimir loved his little cabin and each piece of furniture in it because it had all been made especially for him.

"Then I think we should lay this out. I want to check the ground where we'll dig each footing so there are no surprises." Frankie had seemed so confident, and then he suddenly lowered his gaze. "If that's okay," he added.

Sasha clapped Frankie on the shoulder. "Of course it is. You seem to have a gift in this area. Maybe you should be the one in charge of the cabin project?" He glanced at Casimir. Vladimir worried how Casimir would react. He was always in charge of building projects, but he nodded as well.

Frankie shook his head. "You be in charge. I'll help all I can." He seemed to shrink into himself.

Vladimir slipped an arm around his waist to reassure him. "You don't have to run the show if you don't want to." He wondered why Frankie was so tentative when he clearly had a talent. He suspected it had to do with his memory issues. So much of what he thought of himself seemed to be wrapped up in what he couldn't remember. Not that Vladimir could blame him. That's why he'd backed away from Frankie earlier. He wanted his mate to be sure of his feelings before they bonded forever.

"I'm fine with that," Casimir said. "Let's get to work." He oversaw the other guys, including Tetka and Pavel. They marked out the outline of the cabin, designated the basic features of the design, and then he and Frankie checked each of the foundation piling locations for soundness.

The sun grew hot as the day went on. Frankie stripped off his shirt, and Vladimir found his attention wandering to his handsome, lithe mate. Vladimir smiled as he worked, gaze pulled toward Frankie more often than he wanted to admit. Even Casimir and Sasha noticed, and they were pretty clueless about love. If he hadn't found his mate in Martha, Casimir would probably still be a socially backward bachelor wondering why nobody was interested in him. Vladimir was pretty sure Martha had been the aggressor in that courtship.

"That's looking pretty good," Sasha declared as he stepped back to survey the stakes and markings.

"I think so too," Vladimir agreed, but Frankie seemed puzzled, his lips pursed slightly.

"Something…. Oh. The door is fine, but we need the stove to go in that corner." He pointed. "And the window has to move a few feet over. That way one window will overlook the pack and the other will face the stream. In the winter, the cabin will get more light, and we can put an awning over it so that in the summer, the cabin will be cooler." Frankie seemed to know a lot about building and design. The others nodded as Frankie threw out ideas. It was awesome to see his mate being accepted into the pack like this.

"What's this?" Dimitri scoffed as he strode toward where they had been conferring. "It looks small."

Casimir narrowed his gaze, and Sasha nearly growled. To go further would be to challenge Dimitri, and since he was in line to be alpha, that wasn't a good idea.

"It's the same size as the cabins the other families have," Vladimir explained. "We have windows facing both directions, and we're going to create a sleeping loft. It should be really nice." He was excited and figured Dimitri should be happy with whatever they came up with—especially after their father's outburst last night. But Dimitri seemed unaffected by their father's disapproval.

"Make it bigger," Dimitri ordered.

"We don't have the materials for that," Frankie explained.

Dimitri bared his teeth. "I don't want to hear from you," he snapped.

"That's enough," Vladimir said as he stepped between Dimitri and his mate. "We only have enough materials to build what we planned. We can eliminate the sleeping loft if that's what you want. It was Frankie's idea, and I think it's a great one. But since you don't want anything to do with him, you shouldn't benefit from his ideas." That seemed reasonable enough to him.

Dimitri obviously didn't think so, and he lashed out. But Vladimir had spent enough time with his brother to know his tells. Dimitri was strong, but not nearly as fast as he thought he was. Vladimir easily dodged the blow.

"What's all this?" their father demanded as he strode across the compound, obviously pissed.

Vladimir said nothing but just stood beside Frankie, waiting.

"This little shit is trying to mess up my cabin. He—"

The alpha swiped the air, and Dimitri snapped his lips shut. The alpha looked over what they'd laid out, with Casimir explaining what they had planned. "I think Frankie's right. Maybe…." The alpha's gaze shifted to Dimitri but didn't soften an iota. "Build the cabin with the sleeping loft. Frankie and Vladimir can move in here when it's done. Since Dimitri is ungrateful—*and* under the delusion that he's alpha—he can move into their cabin once this is done."

Vladimir was about to protest, but Sasha shook his head hard.

"I think that's a fine idea," Casimir agreed.

Dimitri fumed, and anger rolled off him like a tidal wave. They could all smell it, including their father, but Dimitri didn't dare say a word. That would be going against the alpha publicly, and there was no way his father would stand for that. Vladimir had to suppress the grin that threatened to burst out.

The alpha took another step toward Dimitri. "You need to do what's expected of you. And I mean to make sure that happens. I'm tired of this enFate's Attractiond attitude of yours."

"But Father... I provide for the pack...," he whined, implying that Vladimir didn't, which wasn't fair.

"Everyone gives according to their talents, and you need to step up." The alpha walked the perimeter of the new cabin, his hands behind his back, and then thanked everyone before picking up a shovel to pitch in with the footings.

BY THE end of the day, Vladimir's hands hurt and his back ached, but he looked on this project differently now that it was to be his. He worked as hard as he possibly could next to Frankie. At one point in the afternoon, the pups bounded over, along with some of the pack youngsters. Unfortunately, they weren't especially helpful, and Casimir had to get Martha to take them back to where they belonged.

"Did your father mean what he said? He wants us to have this cabin?" Frankie asked once the others were out of earshot. "Dimitri was mad enough to spit nails."

Vladimir shrugged. "I don't know. It would be nice." He had never known his father to say something he didn't mean, and since Frankie had been accepted into the pack, things seemed different between him and his dad somehow. Maybe the idea of his son mating had affected his dad more than Vladimir had thought it would. Or, just maybe, he'd actually done something to please his father. Who would have thought it? One thing was for sure: Dimitri was nowhere to be found until the work for the day was done. And then he strode into camp with a buck over his shoulders and a brace of rabbits in his hand, as if to prove his worth after all. Vladimir groaned but said nothing. Whatever happened, this was going to be interesting.

"That dinner was wonderful," Dimitri told the pack members who prepared it that evening, making a big show of getting up from the table. "You did wonderful things with the venison." He spoke more loudly than was necessary.

"He wants everyone to know that he caught dinner," Frankie said. "Maybe later we can go hunting."

Dimitri scoffed. "Vladimir isn't much of a hunter." He smiled and strode away, holding his head high as if he had won something.

Vladimir shrugged. Hunting had never been one of his strengths. He could catch small game when he needed to, but it was his brother who loved the thrill of the chase, the stalking, and ultimately the kill. They were wolves, after all, and hunting was a valuable skill.

Dimitri puffed himself up and sat next to Sasha's daughter, Marika. As the hours passed, Vladimir's father seemed pretty satisfied with the turn of events, so maybe he had gotten what he wanted as well.

In order to avoid another confrontation, not to mention further one-upmanship from Dimitri, Vladimir excused himself and left the pack house, heading for his cabin. He should have known that the whole thing this afternoon had been for show. Sure, his dad would probably let him have the new cabin, but as long as Dimitri did as their father wanted, the alpha would give Dimitri everything he wanted too. Vladimir hated these kinds of games, but he should be used to it by now.

Vladimir only hoped that Dimitri didn't hurt Marika in whatever game he was playing with their father. Marika was a nice girl—quiet and very much like her mother, Liona. He liked both Marika and her mother very much. They worked hard and saw to it that everyone was fed. The only time Liona ever got upset was when things didn't go well in the kitchen. Then the frustration would boil over, and anyone with a brain stayed the heck away.

"That's an interesting pair," Frankie observed as he caught up to him.

"You didn't have to come with me if you didn't want to. I just couldn't stay in there any longer." He paused in the center of the compound, looking up at the clear sky filled with stars. "I'm not much of a game player, and Dimitri is a master." He sighed. Maybe that had been his problem all these years. Everyone around him seemed to be playing at something, and since he had no idea what the rules were, he simply bowed out.

"I get that." Frankie nudged his shoulder. "Did you see him, though?" He seemed concerned.

"What did he do?" Vladimir had obviously missed something. Not like that was unusual.

Frankie shook his head. "You saw Dimitri and Marika. I think she's really besotted with him. She soaked up his attention with wide eyes, and just before I left, your father went into his office. Then…."

Vladmir growled. "Let me guess. Once his door closed, Dimitri was done with Marika. He probably skulked off somewhere, right?" His anger rose. Vladimir knew he was right.

Frankie nodded, and Vladimir figured he should have a word with Sasha the next time they worked on the cabin. Marika deserved someone who would love her for the great girl she was—not a man who was only playing with her affections. The whole thing pissed him off. Maybe he should try to talk to his father too. Dimitri's careless behavior had to stop.

"Let's go to the cabin," Frankie offered, and Vladimir gladly followed him.

The pups were bundles of energy, and Frankie and Vladimir played hunting games with them, trying to teach the young ones to find their own food. All of the pups seemed to have good noses. Frankie hid bits of food around the cabin, and the pups had to try to find them. It was cute until two of them found the same morsel and started fighting over it.

"He's the leader," Frankie said, pointing to the largest of the pups. Vladimir kept them busy while Frankie hid more treats, and then the race was on to see who could gobble up the most. Finally the pups wound down, and Vladimir put out the light, undressed, and climbed into bed.

Frankie followed him, straddling his hips. "Just relax," Frankie said as Vladimir closed his eyes. "I have some oil."

"What are you doing?" Vladimir asked as slick hands touched his chest, slowly stroking along the muscle. He sighed and let Frankie soothe away the tension of the day, stroking his chest and down his arms. God, that felt good, and when Frankie lifted his weight away from his hips, Vladimir rolled over, and Frankie straddled his legs.

Frankie slicked his hands, then stroked his back, soothing away the residual aches from all the digging he'd done that day. The tension associated with his brother also seemed to dissipate, and Vladimir breathed more easily, his mind finally clearing.

"That's it. Let the muscles unclench and allow a little peace to enter your body. Breathe in through your nose and out your mouth." He continued his slow, long motions, taking the pain and anxiety away.

"That's so good," he groaned as his body reacted to Frankie's touch and closeness. Whatever oil he was using didn't have much scent, so Vladimir concentrated on Frankie's musk and rising desire. He moaned softly when Frankie massaged his butt, legs tingling from the intensity of having his mate so close. "Frankie…."

"What do you want?" he whispered back, their hearts already connecting in the darkness.

"I need… I want…." Vladimir shivered, and it wasn't from cold. His entire being longed for Frankie, and as soon as his mate moved away, Vladimir rolled over and pulled Frankie down to him. Their lips met in a slow burn of passion that continued building. He cupped Frankie's butt, holding it in his hands, massaging the firm muscle, collecting the little growls and moans that Frankie delighted him with.

"Me too. I need you. Watching you work and being close to you all day and not being able to do anything but watch you has driven me crazy. I wanted to pull you into the woods so we could…." Frankie paused, and Vladimir placed his hand on Frankie's cheek, the skin heating. He knew Frankie was blushing, and Vladimir found that adorable. No one else in the pack thought anything of letting their desire for their mate show. It was common. "I didn't want anyone else to see. This is about you and me."

"Yeah." He had no intention of sharing Frankie with anyone either. Vladimir felt fiercely protective of Frankie and what they had together. They were special, and what they had was unique and meant only for them to see, hear, and experience.

"Frankie," Vladimir whispered as he ghosted his finger over his mate's opening. His cock throbbed between them, and Frankie shifted on the bed, lying on his back. Without further invitation, Vladimir scrambled between Frankie's legs, positioned himself above his mate, and then slowly entered him. There was never a time in his life that he was more grateful for his sharp vision than right now. The room was very dark, and yet he could still see the ecstasy on Frankie's face as the two of them became one. His lips parted, eyes widening in the ethereal experience that was their joining.

Together, they were like nothing Vladimir had ever experienced. His wolf wanted to howl and cry out, but instead he threw himself into their coupling, taking all that Frankie had to give as well as giving his entire being to Frankie. The experience was heady and life-changing, being surrounded not only by Frankie's body but his spirit as well—something he suspected he was already addicted to.

"Vladdy," Frankie groaned, pulling him forward and deeper. "More, I need more."

Vladimir's instinct was to give him just that. His teeth elongated, and he could feel the blood coursing through Frankie. He wanted so badly to make Frankie his, to take him and mate him forever. What did it matter if…?

Vladimir leaned forward, his lips parting, and zeroed in on that spot at Frankie's shoulder where it and his neck met, the perfect spot to place his mark. It called to him, and his wolf thumped its hind leg impatiently, wanting to take what was his.

"Frankie, I can't…." As much as he wanted to, he would never do that to his mate. Frankie meant everything to him. And because of that, he had to hold off and give him the chance to know who he truly was—to remember everything, good and bad—before they took that final step.

"Are you afraid of what we might find out?" Frankie asked. "Because I am."

His honesty was touching. "No. I will mate you, and I will make you mine and only mine. But I won't do it like this." He ceased to move, though still inside Frankie. "I care for you too much."

Frankie cupped Vladimir's cheeks in his hands. "And that's why I know it's the right thing to do."

Vladimir grinned, his passion building once more. He had never understood just how wonderful it was to be trusted. And the adoration shining in Frankie's eyes was almost more than he could stand. It drove him forward, determined to take Frankie to the absolute heights of passion.

Frankie ran his hands down Vladimir's side to his butt, pulling him closer, deeper, making sure the two of them were joined as close as possible. It was heady being wanted like this, having someone who was there just for him. "My mate… no matter what, you're my mate."

"I am. Your mate forever, given to you by the goddess." Somehow Vladimir felt the link that bonded the two of them together grow stronger. It wasn't a full bond yet and it wouldn't be until they completed it physically, but it was there, a thread in his mind that led directly to Frankie. If he closed his eyes, he could almost see it… and that was probably the sexiest thing that Vladimir could imagine. It took a matter of seconds before the energy overwhelmed him and he tumbled over the edge, bringing Frankie along with him.

Vladimir didn't want to move at all. Frankie felt so good against him that he resisted breaking the spell. But as with so many other things, the outside world intruded—in the form of four pups who were tired of being ignored. They climbed onto the bed, and Vladimir pulled away for both their sakes. The pups had no qualms about attacking anything that dangled. He quickly cleaned himself and Frankie up and settled in the bed, hoping the pups would calm down and take the hint that it was time to go to sleep.

"Have you always lived here?" Frankie asked once the pups had settled in a pile near their feet.

"No." Vladimir sighed. "I spent a few years down below in the bigger city. Harrisburg isn't all that big, but compared to here, it's huge. My mother had an uncle who lived there. I wasn't happy here, so I went to stay with him for a while. He helped me figure some things out. The city is full of people, and everyone is in such a hurry." He slowly rolled on his side, shifting closer to Frankie, languidly tracing the muscle of his lover's belly. "There are cars and buses and motorcycles. I thought my ears were going to fall off, they hurt so bad. All the sounds... and the smells." He smiled. "Some are wonderful, like hot dog carts, steaks, and barbeque grills, but others were awful, like exhaust and gas. It was everywhere. I couldn't get away from it.

"Then why did you stay?" Frankie asked, resting his head on Vladimir's shoulder.

"I think I needed to. I had to figure out what I wanted and who I was. And I did. I came to terms with liking guys, but I also realized that I missed the pack and all the trees and the quiet." He smiled to himself. "I haven't thought about that in quite a while. But I think I needed to know what was out there so I could figure out that what I really wanted was right here." He turned to Frankie, cradling him in his arms. "How about you? What was your home like?"

"It wasn't out in the forest like this, but it wasn't a city either. At least, as far as I can remember. We had a house among other houses, but none of them was very special. Though I do recall running in the woods...." He grew still. "Yeah... the pack had land outside the town that we'd hunt and run on." He shook his head. "It seems strange to have to specifically recall what I should just know."

"Does that mean you can just remember things by recalling them? Is that how you have to get your memory back?" He was trying to understand.

"No. It's just the stuff around the edges that I can get at. The core of my memory is locked away." A trickle of fear ran off Frankie, which gave Vladimir pause. He had been doubting his decision to wait on the mating and wanted to walk back his objections and go forward with it. But Frankie's fear gave him pause. If his mate was fearful of what he might remember, then maybe there was a reason to be cautious. He wondered why the goddess would bring this uncertainty into his life... and then the answer hit him. Maybe what Vladimir was supposed to do was help Frankie get his memory back. But how?

CHAPTER 8

"WHAT ARE you doing?" Frankie asked Vladimir as he rushed about the cabin the following morning. "Don't we have work to do?"

"I thought you and I would ask my father's permission to use one of the pack trucks and take a ride north. There's a two-track road that's not maintained well, but it leads to within a mile of the compound, and we keep a few old vehicles there. I thought we might go for a drive and see if we can find your birth pack. Maybe they will be able to help you fill in your memory."

Vladimir smiled as though he had just had the most brilliant idea ever, but Frankie was instantly filled with dread. "No." He grabbed Vladimir's arm to stop him. "Don't."

"Why? Do you remember something?"

Frankie shook his head. "Nothing specific, just a feeling. I must have walked a hell of a long way to get here, and it wasn't because I took a stroll and lost my way. Something happened. I brought a baby with me." He had never given that fact much thought before. "Maybe I didn't walk this far. I had baby formula and diapers and stuff in that cave. It had to come from somewhere, but I don't know where. I have no clue. Maybe I had a vehicle and it's still out there somewhere? If we find it, then we can learn more about me." The idea had merit. But what if the humans at the mining camp found out about them?

"We can ask Ruck if he knows of anything. He's always roaming the woods in search of food and stuff, especially at night when the humans are asleep." Some of Vladimir's energy seemed to have dissipated. "But we won't try to find your pack… at least not now. Though if we can't learn anything any other way, we'll consider it again. It might be that the only way we can find answers is to go up there."

The words hung in the air like a threat. Frankie knew Vladimir didn't mean them that way, but that was how it felt. The very idea sent a chill up his spine. Something was very wrong with his home pack. The more he thought about it, the more he was convinced it was true.

Still, Vladimir was right—they needed to find some answers. But somehow, he just *knew* that danger lay to the north. And it wasn't only from the humans around the mining camp.

"Okay. We'll do this your way." Vladimir stood, and the pups all gathered around Frankie. They seemed to sense that he was upset. "I'm going to talk to my dad and see what he thinks."

"Are you sure?"

Vladimir nodded. "If I go off on my own one more time, he'll tan my hide, but maybe he'll help us out this time." He left the cabin, and Frankie picked up one of the pups, the little girl, who settled in his arms and licked his chin. He needed all the comfort he could get.

THE ALPHA had apparently agreed that they could talk to "the bear" after the day's work was finished. Frankie thought that was fair, since there was limited time to get the cabin constructed before winter set in. Besides, he was anxious to finish the building too, since the cabin was to be theirs. He liked the thought of him and Vladimir building a home together.

Cando seemed to be waiting for them that morning, and he led the pups off toward where the other youngsters were playing. It seemed that pounce, stalk, and other survival games were on the agenda this morning. Liona was leading them, and she promised to keep an eye on the pups and to help prepare them for life on their own. "Though I don't think it's a bad thing to take natural wolves in the pack. We just need to make sure they stay with us and don't come to the humans' attention. These pups need a safe place just like the rest of us." As would they all, if the humans took too close an interest.

Frankie nodded in agreement as she led the kids off to their games while he and Vladimir walked over to the work site. The footings needed to be finished and the foundation set, two things that couldn't be rushed. Frankie wished they had concrete, but that wasn't something wolves used, so he got more rocks from the stream and used them to line the foundations, then made a sort of mortar out of local limestone that they could use to join them together. Once that was done, they could lay the first logs for the floor joists and then build the walls from there. Mostly, since the structure was simple, the foundation didn't need to be all that deep, and now that the cabin site had been moved, the ground seemed really solid.

"We're going to need a lot of stone," Casimir declared, and the team got together and headed down to the stream to get what they needed to fill the foundation channels and get the stones set.

"And gravel to put between the stones. That will hold everything in place once we start building the cabin," Frankie explained. They all got to their tasks, with Casimir directing the work and the members of the pack putting their backs into it. The only notable absence was Dimitri, who was nowhere to be seen.

"WE HAVE two hours before dinner," Vladimir told him. "Let's head to the stream. I know Ruck's favorite fishing holes. If we're lucky, he'll be at one of them. If not, we can head farther into the territory he roams and hope to find him or leave a message."

"What kind of message do you leave a bear?" Frankie asked.

"A scent mark. He'll know that we want to see him," Vladimir said. "We'll pee on a tree."

"Swell," Frankie deadpanned.

First they checked in on Cando. The young wolf had the pups well in hand and eating out of his. "I'm going to miss these guys when they get big enough to head out on their own."

"Me too," Vladimir said. "But they need to decide what they want for themselves. I think Dad would let them join the pack. But they'll have to meet the alpha when he's in in wolf form and formally ask to be included."

Before leaving the camp, they stopped in at Martha and Casimir's place. Victor was asleep, and Martha sat next to the makeshift cradle, watching him. Frankie knew he had made the right decision. She was going to be an amazing mother, and Victor would want for nothing if it was in Martha's ability to provide it.

"See you at dinner?" she whispered.

"We hope so. Got to check in with a friend," Vladimir answered. Then they left the cabin, heading out into the woods toward the stream.

"I miss being able to come here," he said as they headed north, following the running water that gurgled and whispered as it flowed along its channel. The air here was a little cooler, a little fresher, the trees maybe a little greener from the constant water source. "We used to swim up here all the time when we were kids."

"Now it's not safe," Frankie said, shaking his head.

Suddenly Vladimir indicated that they should be quiet, as he sniffed the air. Frankie did the same, not getting anything other than the earthy scent of the woods and the hint of pine that always smelled so clean and fresh. Vladimir pointed, and they slowed. Frankie tried to see if Ruck was around, but whatever Vladimir had heard, it wasn't him.

They continued forward.

Something splashed in the water up ahead, and Vladimir stilled. Their scent was already heading in that direction. If it was Ruck, he could know that they were nearby. And if it wasn't, then maybe the scent of two wolves would scare off whatever had made the sound. As they slowly pressed forward, there were no further sounds, and Ruck didn't appear. They reached the creek and the swimming hole Vladimir had told him about, but there was no sign of Ruck or anyone else.

"Where next?" Frankie asked.

"There's a fishing spot a couple hundred yards downstream. We're going to need to be careful because we're getting close to the mine. Be on your toes and watch out."

Vladimir led him down a barely visible path through the underbrush. It would be a lot easier in their wolf forms, but they would also be a lot more vulnerable. Right now, if they happened upon humans, there was less for them to be afraid of. At least, that's what Frankie hoped.

"There's someone off to the side. Stay low and don't make a sound," Vladimir whispered softly enough that Frankie could hear, but no human would be able to.

A shot echoed through the forest, and Frankie crouched low and crawled to Vladimir, who had dropped to the ground. He sniffed, thankful there was no blood. Vladimir did the same. Once they were satisfied nobody was hurt, they moved slowly, staying low, toward where the sound had come from.

"It's the same men we saw the other day," Frankie said as soon as he caught scent of them. He would never forget that smell. It assaulted his nose, just like it had then.

Another shot rang out, frazzling his nerves.

"I think I got it," one of the men said, and Frankie wished he knew what they were shooting at.

Vladimir pointed as a deer raced through the forest. Frankie could smell the trail of blood that followed it. The poor thing was wounded, frightened as hell, and had no idea which way to go. On top of that, their scent was probably spooking it even more. A third shot split the otherwise calm of the forest, but the deer was gone. The men took off across the field, trailing the deer.

"It isn't hurt badly," Vladimir told him. "There isn't enough blood. One of them must have nicked it, though. But the bleeding will stop soon, and then they'll lose their trail." He grinned. "And get hopelessly lost. Maybe we should hunt them so they can learn what it feels like." The glint in his eyes told Frankie he was kidding... but not.

Vladimir pointed, and Frankie went off to the east and circled around the men. Then Vladimir sent up a cry, and Frankie echoed it before they moved on and did it again. Instantly the scent of fear filled the forest, floating on the breeze like heavy humidity. Fear smelled bad, and with each howl, it increased. Weapons cocked as Frankie silently made his way back to Vladimir. The two men scampered like scared rabbits back toward the mining camp, with Vladimir and Frankie sending up an additional cry that had the men half running, half scrambling across the forest floor.

"Let's find Ruck before those idiots come back," Vladimir said, then led the way back toward the stream.

Unfortunately, they didn't have any luck. Both of them tried to scent for him, but all they got was an old trail. They tried to follow it, but the path led in circles. Ruck had obviously been foraging for food. "I hope he's okay," Vladimir said as they continued following the trail through the trees.

"How long have you known him?"

Vladimir paused. "Maybe five years. Bears don't have packs. They're more solitary, so once he grew up, he left his family and set out on his own. He came here, and I met him." Vladimir chuckled. "The first time we met, I was in wolf form and he was in bear form. It was tense for a little while, but I could sense there was more to him than just bear. He shifted first because, well... he's a bear and huge. I waited and then shifted as well.

We both got a laugh out of it and became friends. Since his territory is outside ours and he roams farther, he often passes along news and happenings from outside." Vladimir grew quiet, stopping and sniffing. "This way." He raced between the trees, and Frankie finally smelled it as well.

"What is that?" Frankie wrinkled his nose as they hurried forward.

"Skunk to start with, but…." He stopped at the edge of a clearing. Ruck stood in the center, a huge brown bear on two legs, backing away from a family of skunks. Vladimir chuckled. "You got a problem, buddy?" he called.

The skunks hurried away into the trees, and Ruck thumped to the ground, staring back at both of them. Frankie had never seen a bear with a pissed-off expression before, and he started laughing too.

"Come on down to the stream," Frankie said. "We'll help get that off you."

It was awful. But the three of them made their way to the stream, and Ruck waded right in, submersing his big body in the water.

"That isn't going to do much good."

"What will?" Vladimir asked. "I got sprayed once and it was pretty terrible."

"I know," Frankie answered. "The spray is an oil. Peroxide, baking soda, and dish soap will kill the odor. Though it's going to take a while before the entire forest doesn't smell you before they see you."

Ruck climbed out of the water, the scent even worse now.

"I'll go see if Martha has something." Vladimir stripped and shifted, then hurried away in his wolf form. Frankie couldn't help watching him go.

"We were coming to find you," Frankie said, talking to the bear. "I was thinking that I had to have gotten here somehow, and probably not on foot, considering the supplies and things I had for the baby. But I don't know where I might have left a car. I still can't remember, though I get snippets. Vladimir thought you might have heard or seen a car or truck or something." It was a shot in the dark. "Go back under the water and let the current wash over you."

Ruck huffed but did as Frankie asked. Frankie wished he had a brush or something he could use to get the oil out of Ruck's fur.

Finally Vladimir returned, a small bag of supplies tied to his back, and he had Ruck get out of the water and shift back to human. The scent didn't improve, but it was easier to get the oil off his skin than out of his fur, and after a little while, the scent abated and a few bubbles floated downstream.

"To answer your question, I think I saw a car when I was hunting a week or so before we found you. It was well north of here, even farther than the miners. It was in the woods, hadn't been there long, but a lot of the smell had worn off. It could have been yours, but I don't know for sure. I didn't think anything of it. Humans throw all kind of things away when they're done with them. I checked it over for food and then left it."

"We need to find it. It might have clues about where I came from or how I came to care for Victor. I know he isn't my child, but I couldn't tell you anything other than that. Maybe there will be something that explains what happened to my pack." Frankie shifted his weight from foot to foot in a combination of excitement and nerves. Any hints about his past would be welcome at this point.

"I can try to find it again, but I don't remember too much about where I saw it." Ruck sat in the sun to dry his skin while Vladimir got dressed. "Let me see. I remember some berries, and there was some really good fishing along a river. The humans had dammed the flow, and there were a lot of fish that couldn't go any farther. That made for some good eating."

Vladimir grinned. "I know where that is. At least where the dam is. Was the car near the water?"

"A little ways away, I guess." Ruck stood. "Thanks for the help." He shifted back into his bear skin and lumbered off into the woods.

"I suppose that was all we could expect," Frankie said.

"It's best if Ruck doesn't get too involved. He already put himself on the line when we got so close to the mine. We need to figure this out ourselves. Maybe now that we know where to look, we can get one of the pack vehicles and drive up there. For now, though, we'd better get back before it gets dark." They hurried off toward the pack compound.

"SO YOU think this car the bear spoke of might be yours?" the alpha asked.

Frankie shrugged. "I wish I could remember. But it's possible. I had to get to this area somehow, and I doubt I walked with a baby and all the supplies I had with me." It only stood to reason. "We'd like to borrow one of the pack vehicles and go up there. Vladimir knows that area, and I hope the two of us can find it. Alpha," Frankie continued, "please. I really need to know some things about myself." He sat back in the chair. "The small glimpses of my life that seem to come through the haze in my mind are dark and terrible." He swallowed.

Vladimir's father stood and came around the desk, then sat in the chair across from his. Vladimir stood behind Frankie, placing his hands gently on his shoulders in a silent show of his support.

"Tell me," the alpha said gently.

"Well. I know my father hated me for being gay. He didn't understand. The last thing I remember is him telling me that I was a disgrace and that if it was up to him, he'd have me exiled." Frankie shook. "My father said that. But I know, somehow, that I didn't leave after that. I stayed with the pack." A tear ran down his cheek. "Not because my father changed—I doubt he ever did—but I had another reason to stay. I don't know what that is. I wonder if it was Victor, but I…."

"I know. You can't remember." The alpha took his hand. "I want you to close your eyes and think only of me. Concentrate on the sound of my voice and let me try to connect with your mind." He grew still, his voice calming. Frankie knew he could trust it. "Just try to let go and free your mind."

"I am…." It wasn't the easiest thing to do.

"Put yourself in my hands. You need to trust me. I won't be able to read your mind as much as feel your emotions." He continued holding Frankie's hand, and slowly some of the mental knots in his head began to unwind. "That's much better." He seemed so calm. Frankie let go and allowed the alpha to feel what he did. The alpha seemed to come closer, his mind and Frankie's sort of blending, though not for long. Then the alpha released his hands and the connection was gone, like a lightbulb flickering out.

"I'm sorry," Frankie said.

"No, son. It was lucky we got anything at all. The only reason I think I could do it is because we both have a connection to Vladimir." He sat back in the chair. "Whatever happened to your memory, it was dark. That's all I could sense. I tried probing at the closed-off sections of your mind and got nothing. You describe it as a dark spot—I saw it as a wall. And I couldn't get over or around it."

"So you believe him," Vladimir said.

"Yes, I do. And I give you my permission to take the truck. Just be careful. They are registered, and the insurance won't cover any damage to them." He paused. "I take it you have a license."

"Yes, I do. But not with me."

"Okay. I'm going to send Casimir with you in case you run into trouble. But you have to drive because one of these two behind the wheel is not a good idea." He seemed to understand now, and Frankie felt like some of his doubts had fallen away. "You can go tomorrow, once the day's work is done."

"Fair enough." Frankie wasn't going to argue. He stood just as Dimitri burst into the office.

"What do these little weasels want now?" He charged up and stood toe to toe with Frankie. Frankie would have taken a step back, but Vladimir was right behind him. "You know all this memory-loss stuff is crap." His eyes blazed.

"That's enough!" Vladimir's father snapped. "He's shared his mind with me. I could see what his problem was, and it's there." He stepped closer to Dimitri, and Frankie took the opportunity to put some distance between himself and Vladimir's brother. "What has gotten into you?"

Instead of answering, Dimitri whirled on Vladimir and pushed him. Vladimir growled and so did Frankie, rounding on him.

"Don't you see what they're doing? They want to get on your good side, and they've concocted this whole story to make you feel sorry for this one and his little bitch. And you're falling for it. They get the cabin I was supposed to get, and now he's the favorite and I'm out in the cold. I help feed the pack, and what does he bring? Another mouth to feed." He bared his wolf teeth.

"You're full of it," Vladimir growled, baring his own teeth, hand shifting, claws elongating as Frankie watched. "You need to back off and pull your head out of your ass. I found my mate. You should be happy for me."

To Frankie's surprise, Vladimir's father took a step back and cleared the path between the two of them. Vladimir and Dimitri stared at one another, slowly pacing in a circle. Damn, they were getting ready to fight right there in the alpha's office. Frankie wanted to help but knew from tradition that this had to be between the two of them. If he interfered, it could break Vladimir's concentration and cause him to get hurt, and two against one wouldn't be fair.

"I will be alpha here, and when I am, you and your bitch will find yourselves out of here so damned fast, you won't know what hit you. I won't have you two disrupting the natural order of things." Neither of them shifted. Frankie thought that might be taking things too far, considering they were in the alpha's office.

"You wouldn't know the natural order of things if it bit you on the ass. Frankie is my fated mate. That's the natural order." The way Vladimir snapped and stood toe to toe with his brother was impressive, and Frankie's blood raced. Damn, he never knew how sexy aggression could be. Frankie never thought of that sort of thing as a turn-on, but his mate fighting for them— for him—had his blood racing south. "You don't know crap. And if you think you're going to be the next alpha of this pack just because you're the oldest son, you're crazy. No one out there likes you or respects you," Vladimir spat. "You treat everyone like dirt and walk around like you're better than everyone else. The entire pack is working to build a new shelter for the winter, and it doesn't matter if that's for me or Casimir or Sasha or Raisa. We all help each other and work together. That's why I have a place of my own and you don't. Because I actually contribute." Vladimir stood taller. "And I don't care if you're bigger and stronger. A leader has to be smart and have the pack's best interest at heart. You have neither."

Frankie barely kept a snicker from escaping as he realized Vladimir had called Dimitri dumb to his face. "I have the pack's interest at heart," Dimitri argued.

"No, you don't. You're a peacock, all 'look at me' all the time, instead of just doing what needs to be done." Vladimir lowered his arms. "Just go. You're not worth arguing with."

Dimitri's nostrils flared and he leapt at Vladimir. Frankie held his breath as Dimitri hurtled himself forward with all his weight. Out of the corner of his eye, Frankie saw the alpha react, but Vladimir waited until just the right moment, then moved out of the way and let Dimitri barrel into one of the outer log walls.

"Stop," the alpha snapped, and both wolves stilled in an instant. "Enough. Dimitri, you need to back off. I've had it with your animosity towards your brother." He glared, and Dimitri turned, stalked out of the office, and slammed the door. "Well, that was unexpected."

"Just so you know, I don't have any interest in being alpha, Dad," Vladimir said. "I'm happy as a part of the pack. It's where I belong. I know you're a natural-born alpha, but I'm not. Martha would be a much better alpha than either Dimitri or myself." He stepped back, lowering his gaze. "I know what you're thinking, and—"

"Are you sure? You just stared down Dimitri, and he's the one I always thought would take my place. Maybe I was wrong." The look in the alpha's eyes was pure respect. "Sometimes I just don't understand my oldest son," he said half under his breath, as if he didn't mean to utter the words out loud.

"He should never take your place, but I don't think I'm the one to do it either." Vladimir pulled Frankie to him, hugging him tightly. "I did what I did to protect my mate, and no one is going to threaten him or hurt him without coming through me. Not Dimitri… and not you."

The strength in Vladimir's voice sent a shiver up Frankie's spine. He closed his eyes, safe with his mate. Damn, it was sexy to let someone else take care of him.

"And that's how it should be." Vladimir's father sat down and motioned that they were to do the same. "I'll tell you something important. My uncle was alpha before me. He passed away a year after you were born. My cousin Gregor was expected to become alpha. He was my uncle's son and had been groomed for the position since he was a pup. Both his parents doted on him, spoiling him rotten, and he got too used to getting exactly what he wanted. It was a mistake I now see I made with your brother." He cleared his throat as if to dispel the notion. "I thought Dimitri would be a good alpha. He's strong and provides for the pack. I really thought he understood what he needed to do. Anyway, when my uncle passed, the pack rebelled and refused Gregor the position. They knew he wouldn't lead them—he'd rule them as a dictator."

"I've never heard this," Vladimir said softly. "What happened to him?"

"He left after being ostracized from the pack. That wasn't my doing. All the betas and leaders turned their backs collectively and forced him out. He left on his own, and once he was gone, I took over. I didn't want to. It wasn't what I wanted or how I pictured things would go. But my family needed me, the pack needed me, and I had to step up and be strong for them. It wasn't always easy, and sometimes I think I relied on tradition and how things had always been done… maybe too much."

Frankie took Vladimir's hand. "Whatever happens, I'm here with you," he said softly.

"Exactly as a mate should be," the alpha said. "Look, I know this isn't what you may want, but it may be what the pack needs of you. And that's what's most important. Think of Victor and the other pups. They need to grow up in a pack that's led by someone who cares for them and will always do what's best for the entire group. Sometimes that means hard decisions and putting the good of the pack over the wants of an individual. Those decisions are the absolute worst but have to be made. And I'll let you in on a little secret: the person desperate for power and to lead is probably not the one who should do it. A reluctant leader is usually the better one for the pack. He will listen and truly lead rather than simply dictate." He patted Vladimir's knee. "Not that I'm planning to go anywhere in the near future, but I'm also not going to be around forever. And I need to know that the pack will be in good hands when I'm gone."

Vladimir nodded. "Like I said, I think there are others who would be much better suited to the job than me." And in that sentence, Frankie understood that quite possibly the next leader of the pack would indeed be his mate. And like Vladimir, he wasn't sure how he felt about it.

CHAPTER 9

"ARE YOU sure you two want to do this?" Casimir asked as they walked down the path toward the pack vehicles.

"I think we have to," Vladimir said with more confidence than he felt. He was worried about what they might find, and maybe even more about what they wouldn't. If this was the vehicle Frankie had used to get to the area, maybe there would be clues about where Frankie came from and how he got there. And there might even be something that would jar Frankie's memories loose. Of course, there could be nothing… or worse, some sort of danger. "We have to know, Casimir. Frankie deserves to know."

"I don't doubt it. Just asking to be sure." Casimir turned to Frankie. "Sorry for talking around you. What do you want? You're the one who needs to be sure about this."

Frankie stopped and, to Vladimir's surprise, simply yawned. "Yes, I want to know." He had been doing that all day, and the closer it got to them leaving, the worse the fatigue had become. The two of them had had a rather athletic evening, but they had both slept well afterward. "I guess I worked pretty hard today."

"We all did," Casimir said. "You sure you're up to this? We could go tomorrow."

Vladimir shared the concern. They were going to need to be on their toes if they found the car.

"No." Frankie straightened up. "Let's go and get this over with. The sooner we find out something, the sooner we can figure out what my life will be moving forward." He seemed more determined as they reached vehicles.

Two trucks stood inside a roughly built carport. They were largely out of the rain and snow, but the sides were open. Vladimir climbed into the tan truck and sat in the middle, while Frankie drove and Casimir took shotgun.

Frankie turned the key, and the old engine fired up on the first try. He backed out, and they slowly traveled down the rough logging trail. The road had been built some forty or fifty years ago, maybe longer—the last time parts of this area were logged. The ruts were jarring, but the truck was more than capable of handling it.

Vladimir hated trucks. He was much more at home on four legs than four wheels. His belly often got funny when he rode, but he wasn't going to tell the others that. He hadn't eaten in some hours, so he would be fine. Frankie seemed like a cautious driver, going slow over the bumps and ruts until they broke through the trees onto a more traveled dirt road. He was able to go faster then. Casimir guided him farther north, and they passed the entrance to the mining camp, doing their best not to draw any attention to themselves.

"I don't like that place," Frankie said.

Casimir nodded. "I don't either, but the darkness I feel isn't coming from them."

"How do you know?" Vladimir asked. He had felt it too and had thought the men were the source. Mining hurt the trees and the water and, by association, the animals. It was as if the very forest was scared.

"I don't. It's a feeling. They're just miners doing their job. I don't like them and some are stupid, but they're just humans doing what humans do. The darkness is coming from something else." Casimir rolled down the window. "Besides, their scent is dissipating. Maybe they didn't find what they were looking for." At least that was some good news. "There's something else out here, and I think it's more dangerous than the stupid miners with their guns." He sat back, but they all remained on edge.

Casimir continued directing them. "From what your friend told you, the area we need to search should be a few minutes down this road on the left. That would put the car probably three miles from where we found you, Frankie. The roads wind around, but it's a lot less distance on foot. You must have walked and carried your supplies from the car to the cave."

Frankie shrugged as he pulled off to the side of the road.

"Does any of this look familiar?" Vladimir asked. Not that there was anything particularly remarkable about this area. It was forested on both sides of the road.

"Not really."

"Then go forward slowly. If you were out there, then there has to be some turnoff that you took. You couldn't have just driven into the woods. The brush is too thick."

Frankie continued forward as Vladimir scoured both sides of the road.

"There," Casimir said. "We need to check down there." He opened the door just as the truck stopped. "You two stay here. I'll be right back." He jogged across the road and disappeared down an opening in the trees that was barely big enough for a small car. Casimir returned, shaking his head, and got back inside. "Keep going."

They continued moving slowly, checking a few other openings in the trees. They were going farther than Vladimir would have liked. Maybe this was a dead end after all.

"We'll come to the stream pretty soon." They had to, judging by the way the land rose a short way ahead.

"Stop," Casimir ordered as an opening in the trees appeared to the left, along with a glint of metal. Frankie pulled to a stop and turned off the engine. With his keen sight, Vladimir made out the back of a black car. This had to be the one Ruck spoke about. Vladimir followed Casimir out of the truck, and they joined Frankie as they crossed the deserted road and approached the back of the car.

"I don't smell anything much," Casimir said. "It's been here awhile, but not too long. The tires are still intact. They would rot away out here if the car had been here for years." He approached the car cautiously and looked in the windows. "Not much visible, maybe some trash…. There's a child's seat in back." He turned to Frankie. "I'd say we found your car."

Vladimir tried the door, but it was locked. Casimir tried the others with no luck. "I hate to have to smash the windows. If it is Frankie's car, then it would be nice to return to the pack with it in one piece." He turned to Frankie. "Any ideas where the keys might be?"

Frankie shrugged and touched the car… then stepped back like he'd been shocked. "It's my car, and I think the keys…." He bent down and came up with a set of keys from behind the driver's side back tire. He unlocked the doors, then sat in the driver's seat and tried starting the engine. It turned over but didn't catch. "Well, that explains something. It's out of gas. That has to be why I stopped here. But it doesn't tell us why I left the car. I mean, I could have simply walked back up the road to try to find help." He popped the trunk, and Casimir checked inside.

"Nothing back here. It seems like it's been emptied out. Considering all the things you had in the cave, that makes sense."

Vladimir popped open the glove compartment and sorted through the myriad of papers and stuff inside. "It's registered to Franklin Bowers, so it seems that this is your car. I don't find anything here at all about Victor, though now that we're inside, I can smell that the two of you were here before." He really wished the car could have provided them with some answers, but it seemed there was very little to find. "What do you want to do with it?"

"There's a spare can of gas in the truck. That should be enough to get the car back to the compound." At least it was a start. Frankie sat slumped in the driver's seat, his shoulders hunched.

"I was really hoping to find something. But we're no closer than we were before."

"That isn't true," Vladimir said, sliding in the passenger seat and taking Frankie's hand to comfort him. The need to make his mate feel better nearly overwhelmed him. "We found your car, so we now know for sure how you got here. We also know you had to have made multiple trips to the car to get everything out of it, but that you were determined to leave it. My guess is that you wanted to get away from it." He turned to Casimir. "Let's lock the car up once more and leave it here. We know where it is and can come get it later." Something told him that was the safest thing to do, especially considering the way that Frankie had been attacked.

Casimir didn't seem convinced. "You sure?"

"Yeah. We know where it is, and we'll take the keys and can bring gas when we come back." He wished the car had told them a little more, but that was the way it was. Why had Frankie fled his home pack in the first place? And who had attacked him and left him for dead? "Let's get out of here." He climbed out of the car and closed the door, looking around, knowing that Casimir was scenting the air as well.

Vladimir didn't like the scent in the air. There wasn't enough for him to get a good read, but as he climbed in the truck with the others, he was happy to leave it behind.

"Let's go," Casimir said, and fortunately Frankie took the hint, turning the truck around and quickly heading back down the dirt road.

"DID YOU find out anything?" the alpha asked when they walked back into the compound.

"Not much, sir," Frankie reported. "It was my car, though, and I remember it now."

"There wasn't much in it other than a few papers and the registration, which had an address on it." Vladimir handed it over to his father. "Maybe this will tell us something."

"Did the visit help your memory?" Vladimir's father asked.

Frankie shrugged. "Maybe a little. I remembered the car, but not getting here. It's like my memory is only giving up information when I come in direct contact with something."

"Does this address mean anything to you?" the alpha asked, showing the paper to Frankie. Vladimir watched as Frankie went from confused to wide-eyed. Maybe they should have thought to show him the papers before.

"Yes. That's where I lived with my pack. That's the address of the pack house. God, I remember… at least something. My father was really angry with me, but I stayed because my father wasn't the alpha, he was a beta wolf—strong and bossy, but not the one making the decisions." Frankie seemed relieved and then sighed. "That's about all. It's like the wall moved back a little bit, then stopped again. What's wrong with me? These are my memories, and I should be able to get to them. I'm not dumb, and yet I feel so stupid."

"It's okay. We'll figure it out. The important thing is for you to keep trying to get at what's missing. Part of you seems to want to give it up, but something is fighting it." Vladimir was just as frustrated as Frankie. "Maybe we should figure out what might cause something like this." He turned to his father. "It can't be natural. There has to be something else at work here. Maybe Raisa can help us figure it out." He was running out of ideas and hoped the pack's wise woman might have some.

FRANKIE LEFT the pack house right after dinner. Vladimir spent some time speaking with Raisa, hoping she might have some ideas about what they could do to help restore Frankie's memory. "It's like it is actively being suppressed."

Raisa nodded. "I'm not as familiar with this sort of thing as I am with healing more physical wounds. But from what I know and what my mother taught me, memory issues can be caused by one of two things. Some are self-inflicted—something so traumatic happens that a person blocks it out. But that usually has something to do with the incident itself. The attack on Frankie could have hurt his ability to remember, but I thought that he would remember things on his own once he healed and grew stronger." She bit her lower lip.

"So you think it's something else? The second thing?" Vladimir asked.

"I do. But that's the difficult option. This—us, what we are—is magical. The blending of wolf and man into something different, something between the two, makes us unique. We're close to the gods, and they touch us with some of their power. That's what gives us the ability to shift. At least, that's how my mother explained it. We're not men, and we're not wolves, but a little part of both, and that's rather miraculous." She smiled slightly. "But that also means that there is magic in the world—and we have the ability to tap into the power of the goddess and the world around us."

"I understand that." Vladimir felt his patience wearing thin, but he knew she would tell him what she had to say in her own time.

"That means that power, that ability to tap into the beauty of the goddess, can be used for bad purposes as well." Her expression turned dark. "And once someone goes down that path, there is no turning back. Using the goddess's gifts for bad things puts a wolf out of favor and means they can't return to the light."

Vladimir leaned closer to where she sat on the sofa in the room where the pack usually gathered. The others had all left for their cabins, putting the two of them alone. "What are you saying? That someone may have put a spell on him or something?"

"It's possible. Someone may have used something dark—something that would put them out of favor with the goddess—to prevent Frankie from remembering parts of his past. The thing is, spells like that aren't exact, so it clouded large parts of his memory."

Vladimir cleared his throat. "So what you're saying is that Frankie might know something that's bad for someone else." This entire situation was becoming more confusing all the time.

She nodded. "There are so many overlapping issues here that it's hard to figure out." She took Vladimir's hand. "Why would someone bother to mess with his memory? Why not just kill him? They came close enough—they could have finished the job," Raisa said. "Of course, maybe the spell didn't work as well as they thought it would. Frankie did begin to remember things right away, and his memory seems easy enough to jog when he sees evidence. It's just a matter of bringing him in contact with the right things and he remembers. So maybe whoever is behind all this figured they needed to get rid of him permanently. And that was why he was attacked." She sounded like she had everything all worked out.

But Vladimir wasn't so sure. He was wondering if the attack and the memory issues were completely separate. "Thank you for everything," he said. "I think I have something to go on."

"You do?" Raisa asked.

"Well, maybe we can figure out when his memory issues started. That might tell us something." He had some things to talk over with Frankie. Vladimir leaned over Raisa, kissed her cheek, and then hurried out of the pack house, heading to their cabin.

The pups greeted him with excitement, running around the room as he walked in. Frankie sat on the side of the bed, staring down at his feet. "I don't want to talk, okay?" Frankie didn't move. "I don't know what's wrong with me, and I can't seem to figure it out." He finally lifted his gaze. "Maybe I'm permanently broken. You don't deserve someone like that."

Vladimir sat down next to him, threading their fingers together. "You're my mate, and that's all there is to it. You can try to fight it, but if you leave, you'll only be pulled back here. We've met and we know each other. There's nothing that you could do to break that now. You know that. I'll never have another mate—you're it." He leaned against Frankie's shoulder. "If you want to make things different, then it's up to you and me to make that happen. We'll figure this out."

Frankie nodded.

"I was wondering… do you know when you lost your memory? Was it before you arrived here or after?"

Frankie lifted his gaze. "I don't remember much before you all found me. So I think I lost my memory about that time." He sighed. "No, wait… I remember taking care of Victor in the cave and finding the pups. All of that is pretty clear. I was worried about what I was going to do when I ran out of stuff to feed Victor." Frankie began to shake, and Vladimir put an arm around him. "I was scared and alone and… I didn't know what had happened to me. I couldn't remember anything about my life, and I was only trying to survive."

Vladimir patted Frankie's hand. "That means you lost your memory sometime before or just after you left your home pack. And it's possible that they followed you."

"Maybe. But then why aren't they still here?"

"Because they probably think you're dead. You would have been, if Ruck and I hadn't found you. The silver wouldn't have allowed you to heal. It would have been a matter of time before you died." The words alone sent a stab of loss running through him.

"Maybe, but I don't know. That's just it. I don't remember any of it."

"You must have fought them," Vladimir said.

Frankie nodded. "I'd like to think I did." He lowered his gaze once again. "I can't remember much about it. Yes, I fought, but...."

"Concentrate on who you were fighting," Vladimir said softly. "Don't worry about anything else. Were they wolves?"

Frankie nodded, closing his eyes, his expression a mask of concentration, as if what he was doing was painful. "There were three of them, I think. But I didn't recognize any of them. Not even their scent." He shivered, and Vladimir held him.

"You did good."

Frankie held his head and clung to him. "It hurts so much." He breathed deeply, and Vladimir comforted him. "It's better now."

"So when you probe the areas of your memory that are clouded, you hurt?" Vladimir asked.

"Yeah. Sometimes. Pressure builds up in my head, and it feels like my brain is going to explode." That

was new information, and Vladimir filed it away to tell
Raisa. Maybe that would have meaning to her.

"But you did good. The wolves who attacked you
weren't from your old pack, and they weren't from
this one."

Frankie shrugged. "I didn't say that. I didn't recognize their scent because they didn't have one. It was
like it was stripped away. I know it was no one here,
because none of the wolves in your pack are like that.
But it could have been someone from home. I don't
know. It happened fast. We fought, and then there was
so much pain… and then darkness took over. That's
about all I know." Frankie clung tighter to him. "Please
don't make me try to remember more. Not now. I don't
know what happened. All I can remember is trying to
lead them away from the cave. I heard them and led
them away, and they attacked me."

"And once they were gone, you tried to get back,"
Vladimir said.

Frankie nodded. "I had to get back to the pups and
Victor. I figured I could try to get the knife out myself
and then maybe rest and heal. But I didn't make it."

"And we found you." That was all the information
he was likely to get, and it put them no closer to knowing who was behind his mate's problems. Vladimir
continued holding Frankie until he relaxed. "Do you
want to lie down?"

Frankie nodded, and Vladimir let him lie on the
bed. Then he turned out the lights and joined Frankie.

"I'm sorry you're hurting." He slipped his arm
around his waist, tugging him closer.

"I know. I just wish I could remember everything,
and then maybe all this would go away." The darkness settled around them. "Everything is my fault. The

pack here has been welcoming, and your father is a good alpha."

Vladimir hummed his agreement. "I never thought he was bad, just that he favored my brother and was blind to his behavior. But it seems I had things wrong." Vladimir wished he could help his mate. "Just relax. I hope we can figure out the key to your memory soon, if for no other reason than it will let you rest easier."

Frankie slowly rolled toward him. "But what if it comes back and I remember that I'm a total asshole? What if I've done bad things?" He swallowed.

"Your past doesn't matter. It's who you are and the wolf you want to be—that's what's important." Vladimir had to put his faith in the goddess and the fact that she wouldn't give him a mate that was wasn't right for him. "Is this fear talking?"

Frankie nodded and rested his head on Vladimir's shoulder. "I don't remember. But some of the things I feel and can't quite seem to reach are very dark. It's like they're there—I know they are—and yet if I try to dig deeper, all I get is fear and anxiety in return. Maybe I'm not a good person? Maybe I deserved the things my father said to me? I don't know. Maybe it's best that I don't even try."

"And maybe whoever cast the spell that clouded your memory wanted you to think you were bad, so they left those memories for you to find. We don't know enough about what's going on here to make any judgments." An idea was forming in his mind. He had been trying to avoid it for as long as possible, but he didn't think they had much choice now. "Maybe we need to visit your home pack and get the lay of the land there."

Frankie went stiff. "I don't think that's a good idea." From his reaction, that was the understatement of the century. Frankie's heartbeat quickened until it raced. "We can't do that. What if there's danger there? I know that I had to get away from them. What if they're the ones who tried to have me killed?" He moved closer. "I'd rather never get my memory back than put you or anyone here in jeopardy. You all have stayed by me and cared for me. I don't want anyone hurt." He sat up, his gaze boring into Vladimir's. "I don't want you hurt… or worse."

"It's only a suggestion," Vladimir said. He wasn't going to force Frankie to go back. If it caused him that much anxiety, it wasn't worth it unless they were totally out of options. Maybe they would have to get used to Frankie's memory being spotty. There were worse things, and it was possible that his memories would return with time. All they had to do was be patient. But he had a feeling that wouldn't be the case, and something told him that doing nothing wasn't going to help. Still, if taking action caused more harm….

"Please don't. All I know is that I left my home pack for a reason." He shivered, and the pups jumped up on the bed to join them. They whined and then settled around Frankie.

"Guys," Vladimir said softly, placing the pups back on the floor one by one before rolling over and pulling Frankie close. "I won't do anything to hurt you, but we may not have a choice. If we don't find out what's locked in your memories, then whoever hurt you could return to finish the job. And they'll find the entire pack."

Frankie sighed and nodded. "Okay. We'll talk to your dad and see what he says. But I don't want anyone doing anything that will put the pack in danger. Not on my account." He snuggled closer, and Vladimir held him until his troubled mate finally fell asleep.

"I REALLY don't like this idea," Vladimir's father said. "It's a long way, and there's nothing we can do to keep either of you safe. Being gone for a few hours is one thing, but days is another."

Vladimir glanced at Frankie, hating the satisfied smile that formed on his lips.

"Then again, we need to know if there is additional danger." He seemed to be weighing his decision carefully, not that Vladimir would expect anything else. Finally he cleared his throat. "I think we need to remain safe and have everyone close for now. There have been new people arriving at the mining camp, and Casimir reported today that many of them are venturing into the woods to hunt. If they decide to come this way, we are going to need as many wolves to defend our pack as possible."

Vladimir didn't like his father's answer, but he couldn't blame him. "I understand."

"I wish they would discover whatever it is they want and leave," his father said. "They're looking for gold, only there hasn't been any in the stream for a generation or more. Our people once mined the stream for gold, and they used it to pay for things the pack needed, but that ran out some time ago. There wasn't all that much to begin with. I'm sure these miners will eventually learn that for themselves and then they will leave, as others have before them."

"But what if they do find something?" Frankie asked.

Vladimir saw an unusual moment of self-doubt in his father. "Then they'll stay, and we'll have a more permanent threat. Dimitri is trying to convince me that we need to take action against them to discourage their efforts and get them to move away."

Frankie cleared his throat. "Any action you take will only be met with more force. They'll bring in more people to fight us because they won't want to lose. I agree with your previous decision. It's best to hope their efforts come to nothing and they go away." Frankie moved closer to Vladimir.

"But in the meantime, none of us are safe," Vladimir protested. "They took a shot at Ruck the other day, and they could decide to go after any of us. What about the pups? Are they going to be able to run in the woods?"

"I don't know," Frankie admitted. "But your dad is right. We all have to protect ourselves. That has to come first for all of us. If the pack isn't safe, then we can't do anything." Frankie clenched Vladimir's hand.

"You just don't want to go," Vladimir challenged him without heat. There was no use in fighting both of them. He was smart enough to know he wasn't going to win.

"We'll keep that in our back pocket," his dad said. "For now, take care of your mate and keep working on things here. Cooler weather will be on all of us before we know it, and that cabin needs to be built and ready for you to move in well in advance." There was something hard in his father's eyes, and Vladimir knew he had no choice but to agree, even if he wasn't convinced this was the best course of action.

CHAPTER 10

THE PUPS were getting big enough to be on their own, and they loved being outside. The others took turns showing them how to hunt and letting them run with the pack, which was great for them. Victor was growing quickly and had already said his first word. The entire pack had fallen in love with the little guy, and Martha adored him. So did Frankie, but for all practical purposes, she was his mother, and Frankie deferred to her. Victor was a happy, healthy, slightly plump little boy who was blossoming with her and Casimir.

The cabin was coming along great, and maybe he and Vladimir could move in soon. He liked the cabin they had, but it was small for the two of them, and when the pups were there, it was downright tiny.

Frankie stepped out of the cabin on a crisp late summer morning. The cool weather was definitely on its way. Even though there wasn't a cloud in the sky and the day would be warm, the hint of a new season in the air was enough to tell everyone fall was on its way.

"Morning," Sasha called as he hurried toward them. "Is Vladimir still inside?" The door opened, and Vladimir joined him. "Both of you need to come with me," Sasha said.

"What's happened?" Vladimir asked.

"Your bear friend apparently knocked on the pack house door this morning, and the alpha was a little taken aback. He asked for both of you and insisted that we come and get you. The bear—"

"His name is Ruck," Vladimir interrupted gruffly, already heading toward the pack house.

"He's a good person," Frankie added.

Sasha huffed. "He came right into the compound and didn't ask permission or anything,"

"He's a bear, Sasha. He could rip you apart with a single swipe of his paws. And he's my friend and has helped the pack before." Vladimir picked up his pace, and Frankie hurried to keep up with him until they got inside. The entire pack had gathered in the common area, the group buzzing with excitement.

Frankie and Vladimir approached Ruck and the alpha, though Sasha stayed back with the others, close enough to intervene if necessary.

"Ruck," Vladimir said, pulling the big bear into a hug. Frankie realized this was Vladimir's way of letting the pack know that Ruck wasn't a threat to any of them. Still, he wasn't happy about his mate hugging someone else. He had to stop himself from intervening. "It's good to see you." Vladimir stepped back, and Frankie found he could breathe again.

"I wish it was under better circumstances," Ruck said gravely. "I know you went back to the car a while ago, but I came across something I thought you needed to know." He lowered his voice. "I was back hunting up there… and I saw wolves sniffing around the car. They were in human form, but I was able to smell what they really were."

"How many?" Vladimir asked.

"Three. They were wolves, but they smelled different from all of you—more clinical, as if something had been used to try to mask who they were. They also talked a lot, and I heard them mention you, Frankie. They were looking for you. They knew the car was yours, and they were trying to determine which way you had gone, but the trail was long cold, and they got nowhere."

"When was this?" Frankie asked.

"Yesterday. I came back here to let you know," Ruck said. "Even though the welcome left something to be desired." He made for the door. "I'll be on my way now." Ruck turned back to the alpha. "Don't worry, I'll return to my own area and not darken your doorstep again." He lumbered toward the door and pulled it open.

"Alpha," Vladimir snapped, and then turned to Ruck. "Please wait." He returned his gaze to his father. "Ruck came here to warn us of possible danger. He's a good friend, and this isn't how we treat people who are trying to help us." The tone in his voice was deep, rough, with a touch of anger.

"But he isn't one of us," the alpha growled.

"We have miners camped near our territory and strange wolves searching outside our woods, and you're worried about whether someone willing to help us is a wolf or not? Since when do we discount our friends and supporters? When did we get so arrogant that we can't appreciate aid, no matter who is giving it to us?" Vladimir was doing a good job of shaming his father.

All eyes were on the alpha. The way he went was how the pack would go and how they would treat Frankie and Vladimir's friend going forward.

"Yes. Ruck, is it?" The alpha took a single step closer. "Thank you for coming here to warn us. Your efforts and thoughtfulness are appreciated." He held his head high, and to Frankie's surprise, Ruck bent his head slightly to the right as a show of respect.

"I help my friends," Ruck said and then left the pack house.

Frankie hurried out after him. "Thank you for letting us know. Were they the same wolves you smelled the day I was attacked?"

Ruck looked at him as though he had never thought of that. "No. They were different. They were trying to find you, but that's all I know."

Vladimir joined them, slipping his arms around Frankie's waist. "Thank you."

"Yes. Thank you. Come visit any time. You'll be welcome."

Ruck huffed. "I don't think your father would agree with that." He turned to leave.

"You'll be welcome," Vladimir reiterated. "Friends of the pack are always welcome here. That's been a rule in our pack for a very long time. My father just needed to be reminded of that."

Ruck didn't seem convinced.

"We mean it," Frankie added, leaning into Vladimir's embrace. "You are welcome here, and your help has been appreciated, even if some of the other wolves don't realize it yet. We are neighbors, and we all need to help each other or else none of us are going to survive." There were too many threats all around for them to alienate other packs. He and Vladimir needed to fully convince the alpha that they couldn't go it alone. "Thank you for coming."

"What are you going to do?" Ruck asked. "Those wolves were just there yesterday."

"Are they still in the area?" Vladimir asked.

Ruck shrugged. "I don't know. I listened to them, and they smelled me, I'm sure, and hurried out of there. I did the same and returned to my own area. You could try to see if they came back to the car."

Frankie turned to look at Vladimir. He was so unsure of what to do. They weren't the same wolves that had attacked him, Ruck was sure of that. He thought they might have been the chemical-smelling wolves from the mining camp.

"I say we talk to my father, get a group of wolves together, and hunt them down. See what they want and either scare them away for good or get some answers."

Frankie reluctantly nodded his agreement. He was getting tired of not knowing, and staying here wasn't going to get them anywhere. They were going to have to search for what they needed. At least this was close to home and the pack instead of going all the way back to New York. "I think we should go."

"You do?"

Frankie shrugged. "I guess so. But we're going to have to have some force in case they're hostile."

A cry went up from the other side of the pack house, and Vladimir took off around the side of the building, Frankie right behind him. They rounded the second corner just as three wolves strode into the compound. "I guess we don't need to go looking for them."

The pack filed out of the house, gathering around the strangers as Alpha Corelia came forward. He stood tall, muscular, the image of power. "What do you want?"

The first wolf stepped forward. "We've been following the trail of one of our pack members. We found his car yesterday and…." He turned. "Frankie," he called and took a few steps in his direction.

Frankie backed away, and the pack closed the gap around him and Vladimir.

"Like I said, what are you doing here and what do you want with my son's mate?" The alpha stepped in front of him. "I want some answers… now."

"Frankie and I are pack mates in New York. The three of us were sent to bring him home." The wolf's gaze zeroed in on him, and Frankie shivered. There was something cold in those eyes. This wasn't someone he had been friends with. "There's no need to make this an incident between our packs. Our alpha sent us to find and return him to the pack, along with the pup, Victor." He stood straight and tall as though trying to intimidate Vladimir's father. "If you return both of them to us, we'll take them home and leave all of you in peace."

That told Frankie all he needed to know about these wolves' intentions. They weren't friends of his.

"Frankie is part of my pack now. He has found his mate, and they intend to stay here with us. He has petitioned for membership, and it was granted at the last full moon. Frankie is part of us now and you have no claim on them." The alpha stepped forward. "I suggest you and your friends turn around and go back where you came. There is nothing for you here."

"We won't leave without our pack mate," one of the other wolves snarled.

Sasha and Casimir came forward, flanking their alpha, teeth bared, with Martha beside her husband.

"You're outnumbered, and you have no claim here. Frankie has made his decision, and he's been welcomed here. Go back and tell your alpha that he is happy, mated, and doing well. Also inform your alpha that he is to send no more people to look for him and that all contact with Frankie is cut off. Frankie has left his pack and is no longer your alpha's responsibility." The power rolling off their alpha was palpable.

"He doesn't see it that way."

"Do you remember any of these guys?" Vladimir whispered into his ear.

Frankie shook his head. "I've never seen them before." He was certain of that. Every time he encountered someone or something familiar, part of his memory returned. These three wolves sparked no recognition at all.

"They seem to know you," Vladimir observed.

"Maybe from a picture or something."

"You need to go now. We aren't giving up Frankie or Victor. Besides, how do we know who you are?" The alpha's voice shook with power that Frankie had never heard from him. He watched the three intruders, their expressions not as confident anymore. Doubt and tentativeness colored their movements and the way the three dark-haired men looked at one another. They'd clearly thought this was going to be much easier. The alpha and his party moved forward, and within a few seconds, the men were surrounded by the rest of the pack.

"What are you doing?" the leader of the intruders asked.

"We gave you a chance to leave, and now you're surrounded. Put down any weapons and sit on the ground."

"This is going to get interesting," Vladimir said quietly as the wolves did as they were told.

"We aren't here to hurt anyone," the lead wolf said.

"Then why did you parade into our compound, demanding that we turn over two of our pack members, if you didn't expect trouble?" Frankie held Vladimir's arm as they broke into the center of the circle, his mate staring at the three wolves. Nervousness and fear washed off all three of them, and Frankie placed his hand on Vladimir's shoulder.

"There's something else going on," he whispered to him. Vladimir glanced at him. "These aren't betas or strong wolves. They're scared. This doesn't make sense to me. Why would they come here if they don't know me?" He wished he could pull Vladimir and the alpha aside and tell them what he suspected. Instead, he stood proudly with his mate.

"Who are you exactly? And why did you come here? Don't give us any more bullshit about bringing Frankie back to his pack. That story isn't going to wash." Vladimir's voice rang through the assembled pack, and the three intruders seemed to crumble a little, their shoulders sagging.

The lead wolf lowered his gaze, finally giving away that he was hiding something. "They have our mates. We were sent here to bring Frankie back and given something of his so we could follow his scent."

Frankie was right. These weren't pack enforcers or betas but normal wolves pushed into something beyond their limits, and now they were stuck. Frankie felt sorry for them. He knew what it felt like to be pushed into things you had no control over.

"And yet you came into our pack, demanding things you had no right to. You say someone has your mates, and yet you came here to take mine." Vladimir was so strong and confident, standing next to his father. "I think you need to explain yourselves more clearly. Who has your mates, and why would that person take them?"

The leader of the small band cleared his throat. "Our pack was small, just inside the New York border. About six weeks ago, a larger pack moved in, challenged and killed our alpha, then declared that we were part of their pack. No one was happy, and pack members began to leave. The smart ones gathered their things and fled in the night. The others, like us, tried to salvage what was left of our families. But there was nothing. After the others left, those of us who stayed found ourselves at the mercy of their pack. They took our mates back to their compound and made each of us perform a task to prove our loyalty. Ours was to bring back Frankie Bowers. If we return with him, our mates will be returned to us, and if we don't…." He began to shiver. "Jason here has a mate and pups. So does Cheever. I just have my mate, Glenna, but she is pregnant. If we don't return with what we were tasked with…." He swallowed hard. "The last wolf to fail watched as the alpha… he…."

"What exactly did he do?" the alpha asked softly, approaching.

Frankie turned away, not wanting to know the answer. But the alpha seemed to be anticipating the answer he received. "Sasha, I want you to make sure these three are fed." He scanned the assembled pack; then his gaze stopped at Frankie and Vladimir. "Then join me in my study. You too, Casimir. Vladimir and Frankie too." He turned and left the assembly, going inside the pack house.

"He isn't going to kill us?" Cheever asked.

"Not unless you give him cause," Vladimir spat.

"It's okay," Frankie told his mate. "What would you do if someone held me?" Frankie knew he'd walk to the ends of the earth and back to try to find Vladimir if he had to. "Let's see what your father has to say."

"I want them as far away from you as possible," Vladimir growled. "They aren't going to take you or Victor. I'm not going to allow it. They will have to fight me and half the pack before that happens." He was rigid with tension, and Frankie placed his hand on Vladimir's cheek.

"I know that. I'm safe here with you. Now, let it go and see what we can learn from these people. They're scared and have been pushed into things they don't want to do." Lord knows there was something very bad going on back where he'd come from. Maybe it was good that he couldn't remember any of it.

"WHAT DO you need, alpha?" Sasha asked once they were all in his father's office.

"Casimir, please bring in the leader of our group of visitors. I need to ask him some questions, and I want all of you to hear the answers."

Casimir hurried off to comply with the order.

"You have an idea what's happening, don't you?" Vladimir asked his father, who nodded.

"What they're describing seems very familiar." He cut himself off when Casimir returned. A chair was brought forward, and the wolf tentatively sat down. "What's your name? You told us the others, but not yours."

"Hayward," he answered.

"Thank you," the alpha said and sat down. "You explained what was happening and why you were here. That your mates were being held. But what you didn't tell us was who was behind all of this."

"Our alpha—though I hesitate to call him that. He isn't like any alpha that I've ever known. He's more tyrant than leader." He quivered in the chair under the alpha's intense gaze. Frankie felt sorry for him. He knew what it felt like to be under that kind of scrutiny, and it wasn't an experience he wanted to repeat.

"His name."

"Romeroff," Hayward answered, and half the room—the older pack members—held their breath. The others watched the rest, picking up on the tension.

"Gregor," their alpha supplied.

Hayward nodded. "Do you know him?" he asked, his fear level rising. He probably thought the man in front of him was in league with the alpha he was trying to escape.

The alpha cleared his throat. "You could say that. He's my cousin. He wasn't allowed the alphaship here and left the pack. He must have headed north and built one of his own." He sighed. "I should have known he wouldn't give up and would spread his brand of tyranny and hostility elsewhere."

"What do we do about it?" Vladimir asked. "Was that your alpha?"

Frankie nodded as a piece of his memory clicked into place. "My father became one of his betas," Frankie said. "I remember now. I hated him even though my father kissed the alpha's ass. He was always watching me and took an unusual interest in my schooling. He even tried to get me to mate with one of the females in the pack. For some reason, he really wanted me to have pups, but I managed to put him off. None of the women were particularly interested in me, so that bought me time." Frankie tried to breathe normally as large chunks of the memories that had been hidden from him raced back. It was nearly overwhelming, especially when his brain seemed to want to recall all of them at the same time.

"Do you remember why you left?" Vladimir asked.

Frankie closed his eyes, sifting through everything that had come back, but that part of his mind was still closed off.

"No. I can't remember that part of things or what happened right before. But I must have left without permission." That didn't surprise him. "But we have a bigger problem now. What are we going to do about these wolves?"

Vladimir's father didn't answer right away. "Find a place for the three of them to stay." He waved, and Casimir took the wolf out, followed by Sasha.

"Alpha, we have to help them," Frankie said.

"After what they wanted?" he asked Frankie, his gaze hard.

Frankie nodded. "Yes." He turned to Vladimir, taking his hand. "They only tried to find me because their mates are being threatened."

"And you believed him." He turned away and walked behind his desk. "I'll admit, he told a good story, but I'm not so willing to believe him right away."

Frankie lowered his head and looked at the alpha. "You told me about your cousin. Do you think he could do something like that?"

The alpha nodded. "My cousin is capable of that and a lot more. I don't want to get involved with him in any way if I can help it. We are far enough away that we aren't going to draw his attention."

"That isn't true," Vladimir said.

"What isn't?" Dimitri asked as he joined them.

"Where have you been?" the alpha demanded.

"Hunting. I left my catch in the larder for dinner, and I saw three strange wolves in the camp."

"We were just discussing the implications of their visit," Vladimir explained. "They came here looking for Frankie. We can send them back, but they'll reveal where he is, and the three of them are desperate."

"Then we give them Frankie," Dimitri quipped. "Let them take what they want, and we can live in peace. He isn't one of us." He turned to his father. "It's the easiest solution. They get what they want and they go home." Dimitri's tone was arctic cold.

"Frankie is a member of our pack. He's been accepted by everyone, and he's your brother's mate."

Dimitri shrugged. "Then send both of them. They can be mates there. Their alpha will get what he wants, and they get to be together." Dang, Frankie was really starting to hate this guy.

"What sort of wolf are you?" Frankie demanded as he stepped up to Dimitri. He'd had enough of his attitude. "You think you understand what's going on. Where have you been all day? And don't say hunting." He inhaled and had to stifle a sneeze. "You smell like gasoline." He stepped back to put some distance between him and the harsh chemical scent that threatened to burn his nose.

"I don't answer to you," Dimitri countered, but he was clearly uncomfortable.

"You do answer to me. Where have you been?" The alpha came around the desk and approached Dimitri, sniffing him closely. "You do smell like chemicals, and I don't smell a capture. There's no blood, and we all know you like to take down your prey as a wolf. What have you been up to?"

Dimitri pursed his lips, saying nothing.

"Go to your room and stay there." The alpha was so angry, his hands shifted and his teeth elongated.

The display of power was so impressive that Dimitri swallowed hard and hastily left the room.

"What are we going to do?" Vladimir asked.

"I have no intention of sending you and Frankie to my cousin," the alpha declared. "Gregor is power-hungry, and he won't stop once he gets what he thinks he wants. He'll only want more."

"None of us is going to be safe from him," Vladimir said. "You know that. No matter what we do, he's going to come after all of us. If we send Frankie, he'll want to know where he's been. If we send the wolves back empty-handed, they'll be forced to explain where Frankie is, if only to try to save their families. If we keep them here, these wolves will lose their mates and cubs."

It sure as hell sounded to Frankie like Gregor had them over a barrel.

"Let me think about it," the alpha said. "All of you, make sure our visitors are taken care of. I need to have a talk with my eldest son."

Frankie didn't envy the alpha that task.

Frankie followed Vladimir out of the office and closed the door behind them.

"These types of decisions are the reason I don't want to be alpha," Vladimir said softly as they made their way out of the pack house. "They weigh heavily on the soul."

"Maybe. But would you want Dimitri making these decisions? He'd send both of us back with them without a second thought, just to get rid of us." Frankie pulled Vladimir around the side of their cabin, then down into a kiss. He needed the reassurance of closeness and hugged Vladimir to him.

"I'm not going to let anything happen to you," Vladimir whispered.

"You may not have a choice. None of us may have," Frankie said. "My old alpha isn't going to stop until he gets what he wants." Frankie held Vladimir tightly. "I don't remember what happened just before I left, but I know my old alpha. He's strong and mean... and ruthless. I have no doubt that he'd hold these wolves' mates to make sure they did what he wanted, and he'll kill them if the wolves fail. Alpha Gregor Romeroff has no conscience. He doesn't care about anyone but himself and his own desires—power and getting whatever he wants." Now that more of his memory had returned, he knew enough to be afraid for everyone here.

Vladimir walked him around the corner and through the door to their cabin. The pups weren't around to greet them, which could only mean that they were out with the others. "Frankie, I...."

"Vladimir, maybe I should go with them," he said. "If I did, then they would have what they want and everyone here would be safe." It wouldn't matter what Alpha Romeroff did to him because Frankie wasn't going to care. If he was taken from his mate, he wouldn't last very long anyway. But he could protect his mate and the others here. Alpha Romeroff would have no reason to look for him. Victor would be safe, and so would everyone else.

"Frankie…." Vladimir tensed with anger. "How can you say that? Do you want to leave me?"

"No. But I want you and the rest of the pack to be safe. In this case, the needs of the many outweigh the needs of the few. If I go…." His throat hurt and his belly ached just thinking about leaving. "He isn't going to stop, and he'll hurt others to get what he wants."

"But why does he want you back so badly?" Vladimir asked.

Frankie shrugged and tried to put the pieces together. "He doesn't like to lose. And I left. I think maybe that was the greatest sin of all, in his eyes, and maybe my father's." Frankie's head ached, but he kept probing the blanks in his memory, pushing and prodding to grasp what seemed just out of reach.

"What could you have done to make him want you so badly?" Vladimir seemed just as frustrated as Frankie.

Frankie tried to think again, but the pressure in his head only increased. "Maybe he really isn't after me. I'm not that special, at least, not to anyone there. Maybe it's Victor he wants. I took him with me." He met Vladimir's gaze. "They did mention that they wanted me *and* Victor returned. Maybe we're assuming that I'm the important half, when in truth, it's Victor he wants for some reason."

"Is Victor his son?" Vladimir asked.

Frankie shook his head. "Gregor has many children. It's part of his creed to spread his essence as far as he can. So even if Victor was his, it's not enough. I think there's something else about Victor that he wants kept within the pack."

"Do you know for sure?" Vladimir asked.

Frankie shrugged. "Of course not. I'm trying to guess and put pieces together, fragments of my life that I don't even know are real. All I can do is try to draw conclusions from the scraps that I have." He sat in one of the small chairs.

"I'm sorry. I can feel your pain, and I know you're trying. I asked Raisa about Victor, to see if she sensed anything special about him, but she didn't. Still, she also said that a lot of traits don't show up until later in life. So we're back where we started." Vladimir sat on the bed, watching Frankie so intently, he could feel it as well as see him.

"I think you and I need to give this a rest for now. Dad is going to figure out what he wants to do. But I know that isn't going to include sending you away. Mates are sacred. And he knows I'm not going to let you go. No way." Vladimir pressed him back into the small bed.

"But Vladimir—" Frankie whispered before Vladimir cut off additional words by pressing his lips to his.

Frankie groaned and pressed upward, desperate for as much contact as possible. All it took was a single kiss for his worries to fly out the window and for his mind to center on his mate.

Frankie loved the moments like this when everything felt just as it should be. The thought of being separated from him was gut-wrenching. "I can't let anything happen to you or the pack here."

"And I can't let anything happen to you, so we're at an impasse. I believe the only way we can resolve this is by me reminding you just what it means to be mates. It means that you're mine forever." Vladimir tugged off his shirt, letting his hand roam over Frankie's chest.

Each touch settled something deep inside him. "You're my mate, and I want you forever."

"But we haven't completed the bond. You could go your own way, find someone else, and have a good life. I'll know you're out there and that I protected you and your pack." It was ripping Frankie's heart out just thinking about it, but it was the only way he could see going forward.

"No. You aren't going anywhere. This is your home, here with me." Vladimir's eyes glowed golden and his fangs elongated. "I won't let you go. If you'll let me, I'll mate you right here and now, completing the bond, because no one is going to take you away from me. And I won't let you leave because of some misplaced sense of justice. We're mates, and everyone here is pack. We support each other, and there isn't a wolf here—other than my brother—who would let you go. We're a pack and we stand together. That's our strength."

The forcefulness in Vladimir's voice sent waves of desire through him. He knew he was safe with Vladimir, and the stronger he was, the safer and more excited Frankie became.

Frankie knew when he'd been beaten, and he gave himself over to Vladimir. He didn't want to go away in the first place. "I'll stay with my mate."

"That's what I want to hear," Vladimir whispered. He sucked at the base of Frankie's neck, driving him insane. He pushed forward, instinct and his wolf pressing for the mate bond. Frankie didn't want to wait either—he was ready—but instead of biting, Vladimir licked and sucked, probably raising one hell of a mark instead.

"Vlad… I want…." He quivered, and his voice broke.

"I know. I do too." He tugged open Frankie's pants and slid his fingers inside, wrapping them around Frankie's cock. The tight grip was amazing, and Frankie rocked his hips for more sensation, his breathing reduced to short pants. His wolf wanted to howl. "I love how you respond to me." Vladimir backed away, pulling Frankie's clothes off. He threw them on the floor. "My wolf loves you."

"So does mine…," Frankie growled as Vladimir got out of his clothes. Then they were skin to skin, heat to heat, a bubble of warmth and passion surrounding them.

"But we're more than our wolves. You are my mate, and we will finalize our bond once we know everything we need to. I don't want to back you into a corner."

Frankie wound his arms around Vladimir's neck. "What if I want to be backed into a corner… and wrap my legs around you so you can fuck the living hell out of me? What if I know what I want? You need to listen to me. You are my mate, and I want it all, to experience everything with you. The good and the bad, the easy and the hard, the passion and love… for as long as we live. That's what I want. So you decide if that's what you want too. If it is, you know what you need to do." Frankie kissed Vladimir hard.

"Frankie, I…."

"Unless you don't want me, then it's time. I am who I am, and whether I ever remember what I've lost or not, I am still your mate and I always will be." He drew Vladimir down, winding his legs around

Vladimir's waist. "Make me yours forever." He quivered, and Vladimir pressed forward, entering him.

Frankie hissed and groaned as Vladimir took him, connecting their bodies, making them one. Vladimir's heart beat in Frankie's ears, and his blood rushed through his veins. He could hear it all. The highs, the joy and excitement, all flowing into him and then back, creating an amazing sense of oneness that was nearly overwhelming.

"You're already mine forever… and I'm yours," Vladimir whispered, pressing deep, sending a wave of ecstasy that seemed to go on and on through Frankie. "I'm never going to let you go." He rolled his hips, and Frankie gasped, locking his gaze on Vladimir's.

"Then bond me to you," Frankie whispered, holding Vladimir closer as his wolf rose to the surface. He had to hold him at bay, but he wasn't going to be denied any longer. Frankie's wolf knew what it wanted and was calling to his mate to bond. Frankie pushed his fingers through Vladimir's hair, feeling his mate's wolf near the surface as well.

The pull between them was intensely magnetic, and Frankie felt his teeth elongate. He wasn't the one who would be doing the biting, but his wolf was ready. Vladimir's had done the same. Their passion continued to build, their breathing intensifying, souls joining together. Frankie felt as complete as he had ever felt in his life and as the tingling began at the base of his spine. He stretched his neck, presenting it to Vladimir, giving himself over to his mate to take… to make his.

"Frankie…," Vladimir said raggedly and then struck, the sensation sending Frankie over the edge of passion with Vladimir filling him with his release.

He had done it—they were mates.

Frankie closed his eyes, letting the combination of sexual bliss and mated happiness wash over him like the white clouds of summer that floated overhead on a warm afternoon. It was perfect and special, and—

A storm slammed into him like a train. Frankie opened his eyes to see Vladimir looking him over.

"What is it?" Vladimir said. "I can sense your surprise and pain. Did I hurt you?" he asked as he gathered Frankie in his arms, pulling them tightly together.

Whatever had been in that emotional storm passed quickly, but Frankie wondered what in the hell it could have been. Something wasn't the way it was supposed to be. He didn't sense that it was coming from Vladimir exactly, but maybe through him.

"No, I'm okay." He needed a chance to figure out what had happened. He held Vladimir in return as his heartbeat slowly returned to normal and the intensity of the moment passed. He was mated to Vladimir, and that couldn't be undone. In Lycan culture, mating was sacred, a gift from the goddess, and no one had the right to overrule it. Frankie didn't know why that fact was so important at this moment, but the thought alone made him feel safe. He was Vladimir's, and Vladimir was his. They were together, bound forever in their hearts and souls. Some said that even death wouldn't separate them and that they would be together when they passed into the lush green hunting grounds of the ever after to spend eternity with the goddess herself. "Just happy," he added as a wave of contentment settled over him.

Vladimir hummed his agreement and then got up. The two of them cleaned up, and Vladimir dressed quickly and left the cabin. When he returned with their growing wolf pup family, the four cubs dropped onto a bed of blankets in front of the cold stove and curled into a puppy pile. Frankie smiled at the way they instantly settled, tuckered out from their day of hunting and playing.

"I'm going to miss them," Frankie said as Vladimir got back into bed. "I know it isn't going to be long before they go off and form their own pack, or find families of their own."

Vladimir rolled over. "Frankie, there aren't any other wolves for them to have families with. We're the only wolves in these woods. Natural wolves like the pups were hunted to extinction in this area of the country. I'm wondering where their mother came from."

"It's possible she migrated down from Canada or something. Maybe she was ostracized from her own pack and was trying to find one to take her in. We know wolves are smart and instinctual, and maybe something in their genetic memory that gets passed down from generation to generation told her that there were wolves here. Your pack has been in this place for a very long time. That may be what drew her here." Frankie scooted closer to Vladimir, his body wanting to touch of his mate's. "I feel sorry for them, though. They won't find mates the way we did. Not unless we do something to bring more wolves here, and I don't know how we can do that."

"When I leave the pack, sometimes I listen to the outside radio. Lately, humans have been talking about reintroducing wolves in this area," Vladimir said.

"Maybe that's how she came here? Could humans have brought her? Or could she have escaped from them while she was pregnant? That would explain why she died, because maybe she wasn't prepared for life in the wild." Frankie mulled it over in his head but came up with no conclusions. "We're going to have to be their pack and watch over them. Our wolves will guide them until they decide what they want to do." Frankie lifted his head, watching the four of them in their puppy pile, closing their wolfy eyes. "I can't just leave them on their own."

Vladimir rolled over, entwining his legs with Frankie's, tugging him into a warm embrace. "Of course we can't. But the life they lead needs to be their decision. The pack will be there for them, and so will you and I, but their life story is theirs to write. They'll figure out their place in the world a lot easier with all of us behind them." He smiled and smoothed the hair out of Frankie's eyes before turning out the last light in the cabin. "Go to sleep. We have a big day tomorrow."

Of that, Frankie had no doubt. There were days that changed everything, and Frankie felt one of those looming on the horizon.

CHAPTER 11

VLADIMIR JOLTED awake in the middle of the night. Looking around, he saw that Frankie was sound asleep next to him, the pups on still on the floor. Voices drifted in from outside, and he climbed out of bed and pulled on his pants before heading out. "What are you doing?" he asked the three wolves who appeared to be leaving the compound.

"We need to leave," Hayward said. "We should never have come here. Frankie has his own life, and we're going to have to deal with our issues ourselves. They aren't yours." He turned toward the woods.

"That isn't necessarily true," Vladimir said. "Aren't you going to hear what the alpha has to say?" He narrowed his gaze, hands on his hips. "You all waltzed in here making demands, and now, when you don't get what you want, you're going to sneak off?" Maybe these wolves weren't worthy of help if they were willing to give up so easily. "What about your families?"

Hayward sighed. "We thought we'd figure out where they were being kept. Once we know that, we can try to get them out and then leave as fast as we can. We have to get away from there."

"That makes sense. But have the decency to tell the alpha about your plan yourself. He offered you hospitality. I'd think you owe him that courtesy."

The three of them looked at each other and then silently turned around and headed back through the compound.

Vladimir returned inside and climbed back into bed, snuggling next to his mate, who welcomed him back into the bed without waking.

Vladimir found it hard to go back to sleep. He kept wondering if the wolves were going to try to sneak away again, and he was terrified Frankie might try to sacrifice himself for the pack's welfare. In the end, he spent the rest of the night barely dozing to ensure neither happened, and was up early and inside the pack house to greet his father first thing.

"I was hoping some sleep would help me see a path forward," his father said, sitting at one end of the large trestle table. "I don't want to send them back to meet their fate and leave their mates at the mercy of my cousin, but I don't want to put any members of this pack in jeopardy either."

Vladimir nodded. "I don't have any answers. But there is one thing that keeps coming back to me. Once they return, your cousin in going to be reminded that we're here and that we have someone he wants. I'm afraid that we're going to have to face your cousin one way or another. Either we go there and take the fight to him, or he'll come here, or send people, and we'll have the fight on our doorstep." It was a decision Vladimir was glad he didn't have to make, though he knew it was ripping his father in two. Vladimir only wished he could help.

"I know. And I don't know what's best for the pack. We could sit here and hope that we're left alone, but I think we'd just be fooling ourselves." He swallowed hard. "I think parts of the answers we need are locked away in your mate's memories. I wish we could figure out a way to get to them. But I also think it's a spell of some sort, and there's no one here who can deal with that. Whatever it is, it isn't strong enough to permanently block his memories, but it takes something more than just effort on Frankie's part to get to them."

Vladimir sighed. "There is something I don't think we've considered. What if the block on his memory was put there to protect him? What if Gregor had nothing to do with it, but his memories were bound by someone else to spare him, or allow him to get away somehow? I mean, the memories return with the proper stimulation, so whoever did this wasn't necessarily malicious. I'm sure Frankie's memories could have been wiped away completely, but they weren't." He leaned forward. "I don't have a clear idea of what's going on, but I can't help thinking that everything isn't as it seems. Frankie was attacked by three wolves, at least that's what Frankie thinks, and three wolves came into the compound. Except if they had attacked Frankie earlier, they would have known where he was and could have tracked him here any time. So I doubt they were behind the attack. Then there are the miners and the threat that we all felt from the north. Now we have the threat from Gregor and the wolves he sent to find Frankie. It's possible that those who attacked Frankie came from Gregor and that was how they knew generally where Frankie was... but why didn't they finish the job?" Vladimir held his head. "I don't know what's what and who's behind anything any longer, but I do know that we need to put an end to this threat from your cousin. And if you ask me, I think it's best to make him come here. We know our own territory and have the home field advantage. We need to stay strong and united."

His father nodded slowly. Others joined them in the common area, and breakfast started. Vladimir knew their chance to talk was vanishing quickly. "There is one other option. The three wolves in camp are worried about their mates. They were going to sneak away and go home to try to break out their mates and get their families away to safety. What if we help them? We could send experienced wolves to reinforce them. Those three know the lay of the land, so why don't we help them rescue their families and bring them all back here? I know there's some risk involved, but I think it's a risk worth taking. Frankie and I could go along as well. Maybe he'd even get the rest of his memory back."

"Is that what you want to do?" his father asked.

"What does he want to do now?" Dimitri snapped as he plunked himself down next to the alpha.

"Dimitri...." The rumbling alpha's tone was a clear warning.

"What? He doesn't know anything. Let me guess. He wants us to go fight your cousin and take him out. You know that isn't going to work. Gregor is too strong and he's too smart." He smiled smugly.

Vladimir narrowed his gaze. "How do you know?" he asked. "What makes you such an expert on this other alpha... unless you've been in communication with him?" He glared at his brother. "You have, haven't you? Those long hunting trips where you're gone for days and only bring back a single deer." He stood up, glaring down at his brother. "How else would you know about Gregor? Dad has never spoken about him, and he left before you were born." Vladimir was livid.

His father was pale. "Dimitri…," he finally said, turning on his eldest son. "What have you done?"

Dimitri jumped up and backed away, but their father was faster, gripping him by the shoulder.

"Don't you lie to me. What have you been playing at?"

"Nothing, I…." He took another step back, but the alpha yanked Dimitri closer.

Within seconds it turned into a battle of wills. Finally their father shifted his arm and pushed Dimitri to the floor in a massive display of power. "What did you do? Don't you lie to me. You have been seeing my cousin, haven't you? That explains so much about what's been going on lately. Your attitude change, the demands, the superior swagger. It all comes from him, doesn't it?" he demanded, holding Dimitri down.

"Dad," Vladimir said as his father went for Dimitri's throat. He could feel the anger and aggression running off his father like rain off a roof and knew this was going to end badly.

"He was willing to betray all of us. Why?" their father demanded, his voice booming off the walls. The last of the others scattered out of the room and the house, the doors banging closed behind them. "What did you expect to gain?"

"I knew my little brother here wasn't going to sit back and play second fiddle for long. Not once he met his mate. I've had the knife for years just in case Vladimir tried to supplant me." Dimitri growled. "He said he didn't want to be alpha, but I knew better. And when I scented his little bitch, I knew exactly who he was…

and what he meant. So I did what I had to do to make sure he never met his bloody mate." He grinned. "And I would have succeeded if three weird-smelling wolves hadn't snuck up on me. I threw the fucking knife and got the hell out of there before the idiots shot me." He snickered. "Too bad the little shit didn't have sense enough to die. But the best part was he was so weak, he didn't even see me. They tore him up and I got away before he knew what was happening."

"So you—" Vladimir found he couldn't speak as anger welled inside him. His wolf burst out of him within seconds, shrugging off the remnants of Vladimir's clothing. He stood in the pack house, fully shifted, growling at Dimitri, ready to take him on. His own brother had been responsible for the attack on his mate. The human part of Vladimir pondered the revelation. The wolf portion wanted to rip his brother to shreds and leave the little pieces strewn all over the forest. The human part of him didn't want Dimitri dead—but his wolf wanted to kill him so thoroughly that the mere memory of him was gone.

"Vladimir, stand down," the alpha commanded.

Vladimir ignored him and stalked closer. Dimitri had tried to kill his mate. It didn't matter to his wolf that it had been before they had met. If Dimitri had succeeded, Vladimir wouldn't have found his mate, and to his wolf, that was just as unforgiveable. He bared his teeth and stalked closer, ready to take on both his brother and his father. His mate was not to be touched, and Dimitri had violated that law.

"Vladimir!"

Vladimir once again ignored his alpha, turning to Dimitri. His wolf had a right to take out the threat to his mate. That was one of the rules of their kind. Mates were sacred, and a threat was to be dealt with.

"Vladimir." A soft voice cut through the welling anger and hatred, soft fingers sliding along his back and through his hair. "It's okay. Your father can handle this." Frankie's eyes and face took up his field of vision. "Just shift back for me." He leaned closer, pressing into Vladimir, the touch cutting through the swirling emotions and adrenaline like a knife through butter. "That's it."

Vladimir's heartbeat slowed and the urge to kill abated as he shifted his attention to his mate. Vladimir let Frankie lead him away, putting distance between them and Dimitri. Then he shifted, and Frankie covered him with a blanket. "You know I won't get cold."

"It has nothing to do with that. I don't want them looking at what's mine," Frankie said as Vladimir pulled him into his arms, protecting his mate from Dimitri.

"That's better. Frankie, take him out of here and go back to your cabin. Dimitri and I have some things to discuss. I'll call for both of you once I have this under control."

Vladimir growled again as his gaze shifted to his brother.

"I'll handle this, Vladimir. You take care of your mate."

Vladimir let himself be led out of the pack house.

"When I woke up this morning, you were gone. Then I felt your anger, so I followed you and found you in the pack house. What was that about?"

Vladimir's teeth elongated just from thinking about what he was going to tell Frankie. "Dimitri was the one who stabbed you. He confessed to it." Vladimir clutched Frankie to him. He needed to feel his mate, to know that he was okay. Without thinking, he lifted Frankie and brought him to the bed. Vladimir stripped him, needing to see every inch of him, to know that he was truly unhurt. "You're mine," he growled.

"And you're mine," Frankie told him as Vladimir dropped the blanket and prowled over Frankie. His wolf wasn't going to be denied his mate, and he only stopped when Frankie groaned and kissed him as Vladimir slid into his body. "Take me. Make me yours again."

HOURS LATER, his mate still asleep, Vladimir got out of bed as quietly as he could. He didn't want to wake him. Frankie had to be wiped out after the way they had made love. Vladimir's wolf still wasn't sated and probably wasn't going to be for a while. Just thinking of what Dimitri had done was enough to get his blood boiling and send his wolf back to his mate, most likely to start all over again. That had already happened twice, and Frankie wasn't up for a third time. He snuffled a little in his sleep, pulling the covers around him, nestling down.

Vladimir dressed and opened the cabin door. The four pups raced in and jumped up on the bed to get at Frankie. "What's going on?" Frankie asked sleepily as the pups tried to entice him into playing.

"I need to speak to my father." Vladimir wasn't looking forward to this, but he needed to know what had happened between his father and brother. "Stay here."

Frankie stroked each of the pups before pushing away the covers and getting out of bed. Vladimir couldn't help smiling at the marks, his marks, that his mate wore. "I'm going with you."

"What if—?" Vladimir protested, but Frankie flashed him a defiant look.

"Don't even go there. I'm going with you, and you aren't going to stop me." Frankie pulled out his clothes and yanked them on. Then he whistled, and the four pups pranced up behind him and out into the compound.

"They're coming too?" Vladimir asked.

"Yup. They're our posse, and we're their pack." He stomped off toward the pack house, and Vladimir had to hurry to keep up with him. It seemed his mate was pissed, and Vladimir had no intention of fanning the flames. "What are you waiting for?" Frankie asked as he picked up his pace.

THE PACK house was silent when he entered. Vladimir had expected some major upheaval or at least the normal everyday activities of the pack—breakfast, conversation, gossip… all the markings of a family. Instead, those he passed were silent, sitting at the table or in chairs, looking at each other as if their world had just come to an end. And maybe that was true, as far as they were concerned.

"Where is the alpha?" he asked. Martha shifted Victor in her arms and pointed. "Okay. Has breakfast been made?" She shook her head. "Then can you take charge of that, please? Frankie and I are going to talk to the alpha, and then once we've had breakfast, everyone needs to get to work." His gaze fell on the three visitors. He couldn't think of them as intruders any longer. "You can help where you can."

He waited until everyone knew what they were doing before pulling open the door to his father's office. "Dad?"

His father sat behind his desk, stunned and immobile.

Vladimir inhaled, wrinkled his nose, and lowered his gaze. "What happened?"

"Your brother...." He breathed. "He challenged me and then attacked. I...." He lowered his gaze to what was left of Dimitri in human form on the wooden floor, blood pooling around his neck.

Frankie bent and checked him. "He's dead," Frankie whispered.

Vladimir swallowed hard, turning as his father nearly collapsed onto the desk. Not only had he killed his own son, but he had done it in his office, behind closed doors. Challenges were public, laid down and settled in front of the pack so everyone could witness the challenge and the outcome. But something like this.... Not that Vladimir doubted his father's story about Dimitri challenging him, but there would be doubts. And they would linger in the pack for as long as his father remained the leader. "What do we do?"

"I need to step down," his father whispered. "I can't.... I should have opened the doors and let the pack hear...." Vladimir had never—not ever—seen his father, the alpha, act like this. His father was confident and powerful. Not scared and... broken.

"We need to tell the pack first. They need to know." Vladimir pulled open the door and asked Casimir and Sasha to come in. They must have smelled something from outside, but the shock on their faces showed that neither of them was prepared for this. He needed to make a split-second decision. "Dimitri challenged our alpha and lost. He was making threats against the entire pack and has been in league with Alpha Romeroff. It was also Dimitri who attacked Frankie in the woods. He was going to betray us all. Please remove Dimitri and bury him off pack land. He's no longer one of us, and it turns out he hasn't been in quite some time."

Sasha and Casimir both turned to Vladimir's father, who nodded but said nothing. Fortunately, they left the office.

"Let's let them do what they need to," Frankie said. Then he turned to Vladimir's father. "Alpha, please. The pack needs you. They're scared and worried."

Vladimir wondered how his father was going to react, but something seemed to click behind his eyes. They cleared, and his shoulders straightened. Then he nodded and got up and left the office. Vladimir was so proud of his mate. Frankie had remained strong, even at a time like this.

"We're going to need to clean this up," Vladimir said.

Frankie shrugged. "Yes. But you realize that your father might never set foot in this room again, right? He'll probably move his office somewhere else in the house. He isn't going to want to work in the same room where he had to kill his eldest son." Frankie came over and folded himself into Vladimir's arms. "Just support him."

That seemed like such a strange thing to say. Vladimir had never known his father to need support. Through his entire life, his father had been strong and wise in the decisions he made for the pack. He ensured that they had shelter and enough to eat. And as the pack grew, he made sure there was room for all. There had never been a time when his father hadn't been in charge. No, Vladimir hadn't always seen eye to eye with his father, and he knew the two of them were not going to agree on everything, but he still hated to see his dad, his alpha, demoralized this way.

Casimir and Sasha returned, and they cleared the room and cleaned away the blood. They wrapped Dimitri in an old blanket and carried it away, leaving the pack house through the door closest to the woods, judging by the slam. "They will bury him, won't they?" Frankie asked.

"Yes." As much as Vladimir hated his brother for what he'd done, he wouldn't let his body be thrown to the scavengers. No matter how much he might deserve it.

THEY SPENT the next hour scouring the room, then shut the door on their way out. The pack had thankfully moved on to their tasks for the day, and Vladimir figured he and Frankie should do the same thing. It was important, in his view, for things to remain as normal as possible. Yes, what had happened was a shock, but the pack needed to know that their lives would continue on as usual. Dimitri had become more of a disruption than an actual pack member, and maybe he was the source of the wrongness they'd felt in the forest. Still, he was someone everyone had known for most of their lives. There was going to be grieving.

The alpha sat at the table, talking quietly with some of the women, the four pups sleeping at his feet as though they knew he needed some comfort. Vladimir went up to him. "We're going to head out to work, but at the end of the day, we should probably talk. Your cousin was actively trying to cause trouble in the pack, and I don't think we can just let that pass," Vladimir mused out loud.

"No. But we aren't going to war either." He lifted his gaze from the table. "I think your idea yesterday is the better one."

Frankie turned to him. "What idea is that?"

"That we take a group and try to rescue the families of the wolves who made their way here," Vladimir explained.

Frankie put his hands on his hips. The glare would have been cute if Frankie hadn't been so serious. "Let me guess. You figured that you'd go with them, right?" He pursed his lips, eyes narrowed and shooting daggers.

"I thought we'd both go. It might jog your memory. Besides…." Vladimir took Frankie's hand. "I didn't figure you'd let me go without you."

"Damned right," Frankie told him.

"Then we should talk to our visitors and get the lay of the land. Once we know that, we can decide the next step." Vladimir knew they had plenty to do before anyone went anywhere.

CHAPTER 12

FRANKIE SAT in the pack van with Vladimir, Casimir, and their three visitors, heading north toward the New York state line. It had taken them three days to come up with a course of action.

"How do we know they're still being held in the same place?" Hayward asked, the other two largely silent, worry washing off them. Frankie kept an eye on all of them, looking for any sign that the strangers could be leading them into a trap, but all he sensed was that they were genuinely concerned for their families.

"We don't. But we'll go there after dark and scope it out. You said that they were being kept in a compound outside the main pack, right?" Frankie said, and all three of them nodded. "It shouldn't be hard to find that and see if it's still being used. We can find out what kind of security the compound has. Then we can put our plan into action, get them all out and into the van." Frankie wished they could have brought another vehicle, but this was the only one the pack owned that would carry more than a few people. On the return trip, any rescued pups would need to sit on their parents' laps until they could get to safety.

"That's the easy part. There are going to be plenty of wolves watching the compound and they will smell us coming."

Frankie smiled. "I thought of that, and I have an idea. The wind comes out of the west, so yeah, we'll approach from the east to minimize the possibility of being detected."

Hayward interrupted him. "That's true and we can do that, but I was thinking that if we used ammonia or bleach, we might be able to confuse them."

"It's possible," Vladimir interjected. "But that would also mean that we'd be slowed down too. There are going to be a lot of wolves and a lot of scents. We'll check things out, make a plan, and then move in fast and get the hell out of there. Nothing elaborate, just a fast in and out using surprise to our advantage."

Frankie nodded. It was the best tool they had. "I found a hotel about two miles away from the compound. It's one of those chain places that's just off the highway. We should be largely anonymous there, I hope. We'll get two rooms. We should be close enough to scout things out from there, though we'll have to be careful not to be seen."

"I know that area," Cheever offered. "There are old trails through there that no one uses anymore. Parts of the area were built up to build the hotels and gas stations, but there are wetlands too. I know them pretty well because I used to play there when I was a pup."

"Then Cheever and I will go look around the area," Casimir said. "Everyone else will stay at the motel and rest so you'll all be ready when the time comes."

"I'm going too," Frankie said, daring Vladimir to contradict him. "I need to see this area. Maybe it will jog something in my memory that can help us."

Vladimir growled as Frankie expected him to. "No."

Frankie slowed down and smoothed his hand over Vladimir's arm. "I need to do this. I have to know if there are answers here for me, and I can't get them sitting in a hotel. If there is something waiting for me, then it's best I find out before we're actually trying to help all these wolves." He picked up speed. "I know you want to keep me safe, but I won't be wrapped in cotton." Frankie felt the anxiety rolling off Vladimir, but he didn't say anything more on the subject. Frankie had no illusions that they were going to be at odds over this until Frankie actually disappeared into the woods. "I'm determined," he added. "You gotta let me do this. We're only going to look and watch. I promise." The anxiety didn't lessen, but Vladimir's expression softened.

It took another hour before they arrived at the hotel Frankie had seen on the map. It was just the kind of place he was hoping for. Lots of people, traffic, and plenty of exhaust fumes that burned his nose but would also help mask their scent. He parked the van, and Vladimir went inside to get the rooms. When he returned with the keys, Frankie drove them all around the back.

"I got us rooms near the back exit. We should be able to come and go with our keys, at least until ten or so. Then we'll probably have to go through the lobby." He passed out the keys, and they went inside.

The hotel smelled of cleaning solution and Febreze, which made Frankie sneeze more than once before they got to their room and he was able to open the window and let in some fresh air, lessening the concentration of the irritating smells.

"When are you going to go?" Vladimir asked, sitting on the edge of the bed. "We really shouldn't stay here too long. It will draw attention. I'm sure some of Gregor's pack members come by now and then. We don't want anyone realizing we're here." He kept his gaze at the floor, which bothered Frankie.

"I'm going to talk to Casimir and Cheever, but I want to go soon and get back before it gets too late. That way we can get the lay of the land and stop this." He lightly touched his mate's chin. "I want this over with just as badly as you do. Then you and I can go back to our little cabin and stay there, alone, for two days." He smiled and leaned closer. "You know, we're in a hotel behind a locked door that no one else has the keys to. The others are resting for a little while." He did his best to leer, but Vladimir didn't rise to the bait. In fact, he barely smiled. "It's going to be okay."

Vladimir wrapped his arms around Frankie's waist. "Maybe I should go with you."

"Come if you want. I'm not stopping you." He rested his head on Vladimir's shoulder.

Vladimir sighed. "No. I should stay here and keep our new friends company. They're getting more and more worried as time goes by. Also, the smaller the group, the less likely you'll be noticed. Just be careful, and if there's any sort of trouble, get the hell out of there as fast as you can. We can pack up and be on the road in a matter of minutes." He held Frankie tighter. "I don't want anything to happen to you. It's my job to protect you."

Frankie chuckled. "How very alpha of you." He was teasing, but Frankie had seen more and more alpha characteristics in Vladimir over the past few weeks. There were wolves who believed that a wolf had to be born an alpha. Frankie wasn't so sure. Yeah, there were characteristics that good alphas had and they couldn't be taught, but the biggest and strongest wolf didn't necessarily make the best alpha. A good one often had characteristics that didn't come with physical strength. They came from character and heart, things Vladimir had in abundance.

Vladimir lightly smacked his butt. "Smartass."

"Just remember that no matter what, I'll come back to you." There was no way he could leave his mate behind. "We're wolves and we mate for life. You don't have to worry about me. I'll carry part of you right along with me wherever I go."

Vladimir nestled closer. "I know, just like I carry part of you. But I hate letting you out of my sight. I want to protect you and make sure no one can hurt you." His breathing grew more even, and he relaxed a little.

"I know you do. But this"—he waved his arm—"whatever is going on, it's bigger than both of us. It's affecting so many others, including our pack. I can't let that happen. We have good people who care about us and support us. I can't let them be hurt because of me. What if there are truly terrible things in my past and the answers that I need are here? I have to try to find them." He closed his eyes, relishing a few quiet moments with his mate.

"I know. I wish I could do it for you." Vladimir tugged him back and carried them both down onto the bed. "But I know I can't. Still, I worry that you're going to remember things that are hard and I'm not going to be there for you."

Frankie adored that fact that Vladimir wanted to help him, but there were some things that a person had to do for themselves. He kissed Vladimir hard, the passion between them building just as a knock sounded on the door. Frankie groaned softly and got up, checked to see who it was, and opened the door to Casimir.

"Jesus, you two. Leave you alone for five minutes...." He waved his hand in front of his face, and Frankie realized the room did smell a little funky. Not that he was going to apologize for it. Having a mate and the euphoria that came with it were things he had always dreamed about. "We need to be ready to go in fifteen minutes. It would be faster to go in wolf form, but it will also be more difficult to communicate, so we are going to need to stay as we are. It's a few miles away, and the terrain is going to be rough and potentially wet."

"Okay. I'll meet you at the back door, then, and we'll go." Frankie was anxious, but it was best to get the task at hand done and over with. Casimir nodded to both of them, then left the room, closing the door without further comment. "I should get ready."

"I brought a small pack." Vladimir pulled it out of his bag. "Take some water and food, as well as dry socks. I know you need to travel light, but you should be prepared as well. There's a small first aid kit too. And switch your cell phone to vibrate, then put it in a plastic bag to keep it dry." Vladimir made sure everything was ready to go; then the two of them left the room and headed for the back door, where Casimir and Cheever were waiting.

"I'll be careful, I promise," Frankie said and then kissed Vladimir. He intended it to be quick, but Vladimir had other ideas. Finally, now a little breathless, Frankie walked across the field and into the woods with

Casimir and Cheever. He couldn't help taking a look back just before the trees closed around them.

THE PATH through the woods was as rough and boggy as he had expected. The trees provided dense shade, with dapples of sunlight showing through here and there. The bogs and soupy areas were interspersed among the trees, and though Cheever led them easily around the low spots, at times they had to pick their way through the underbrush. "Are we getting close?" Frankie asked after an hour.

"Yes," Cheever answered softly. "The main pack compound is about a mile in that direction," he said, pointing. "At least that's where Gregor has his mini mansion. There are homes and other buildings spread through the area. He didn't want our families to leave, so he moved all of them into what used to be an old lumber camp, I think. There aren't any fences, but our people are watched all the time." He grew quiet and pointed at something in a tree. "Motion camera," he said, moving around behind it.

"Are there a lot of them?" Casimir asked.

Cheever shook his head. "A few on each side. They're expensive and don't report back, but they will take stills with movement. They're checked each day, I understand. It's best to avoid them just so they can't finger us."

About a hundred yards later, Cheever crouched down and pointed ahead. He moved toward the east and then forward through the trees. Then they stopped, and Frankie heard intermingled voices.

Cheever lowered his head. "That's my mate," he breathed as naked pain and longing crossed his features.

That answered the question about whether they were still there.

Frankie slowly moved forward, using the undergrowth as cover. He didn't want to get too close, but he needed to see what they were up against.

There looked to be maybe half a dozen dilapidated cabins that made their homes look like a Hilton hotel. Women stayed in small groups with their children, but there was no playing, and the scent of fear permeated the air. This was a terrible place, and Frankie knew they were right to get these wolves out of here. No one deserved to be treated like this. Frankie held his anger inside and forced his mind to assess the situation rather than become overwhelmed by the misery he saw. If he was going to help them, he needed to think.

Casimir tapped him on the shoulder and pointed to a pair of huge wolves off to the side. He pulled a small gun from his pack and showed Frankie the darts he'd brought. Frankie nodded. Tranquilizers were the best way to take them out. If they worked fast enough, they would have time to get everyone away. Casimir pointed back the way they'd come, and Frankie turned to Cheever. He was supposed to be with him, but Frankie didn't see him at first.

Cheever had gotten closer to the camp. Frankie motioned for him to get back, but it was too late. One of the pups in camp had noticed Cheever and started for the woods. Shit, they were going to be seen any minute. Casimir hurried closer, aiming the tranq gun, and fired off two shots. The huge wolves seemed surprised, swatting at the darts before going down to the ground.

"Daddy," the little boy cried, and suddenly the compound erupted into pandemonium.

Frankie swore under his breath, hurrying forward.

"Glenna," Cheever said, and a woman hurried over with another child. "Are there more guards?"

"No."

"Then get everyone. We've got to go right now. These wolves are helping us, and those guards aren't going to stay out for very long." He handed her the other child. "Take the trail out toward the hotels near the highway. Go, get out of here. We'll catch up." They took off, and Frankie, Cheever, and Casimir hurried forward.

"Cheever," two other women said as they raced up.

"The men are safe and back with us."

"Is that all of you?" Frankie asked the group of five pups and two women. Both women nodded. "Then take the youngsters and get out. Your mates are waiting for you." He lifted one of the young ones. "I'm a good wolf, I promise. I'm taking you to your daddy." It was the only thing he could think of to say. After checking that the others were on the way, he herded them all into the woods, with Cheever and his mate leading the way.

They all had their arms full. Casimir carried two children, and the women each one of the others. Thankfully they stayed quiet, probably out of fear.

"This way," Cheever said up ahead.

They all hurried, but carrying the kids slowed them down. Frankie had no idea how long the tranquilizers would last, and the guards would have no trouble following their scent. Their best chance was to get as far away as possible before the guards woke up and realized what had happened.

A wolf cry split the air, floating over the landscape.

"Keep going. We have to move," Frankie said.

They picked up the pace, but with the excess weight, Frankie's legs and arms ached. The others were slowing as well, but they continued forward.

Another cry went up, this one closer. Frankie's heart beat faster as they dodged the low spots.

Frankie knew their pursuers were in wolf form and racing toward them at top speed. Their only saving grace was that they had gotten a head start of twenty minutes or so. Finally they broke out of the woods and made a run toward the hotel. Frankie stopped, and Cheever took the boy in his arms and continued toward the hotel while Frankie slipped off the backpack and called Vladimir.

"Get everyone out and in the van, now."

"What? Why?" he asked.

"Plans changed. We got them, but we're being pursued. Get our stuff and get ready. We need to get the hell out of here." He put the phone in his pocket, wishing he'd thought to call earlier. Frankie grabbed the pack and the keys, and unlocked the van. "Everyone get in the back. Kids, sit on your mothers' laps for now. Your dads will be out soon, and we're going to go." He slammed the door as soon as they were inside, and went to meet Vladimir, who was coming out with their bags.

The reunions were fast as everything was tossed into the very back of the van and the adults squeezed onto the back two bench seats, with Vladimir taking shotgun. Frankie closed the door and started the engine as two huge wolves emerged from the woods at the far side of the clearing. Frankie pulled out of the hotel parking lot and turned toward the south, not picking up speed—or giving them away—until the hotel was out of sight. Then he sped up and made for home like a bat out of hell.

"Is everyone okay?" Vladimir asked, turning around.

"Where are you taking us?" Glenna asked as two of the pups began to whine.

"It's okay," Cheever soothed. "We were sent to find Frankie, but what we found was a pack that was willing to help us." He seemed relieved. "It's okay."

"But Alpha Romeroff, he…," she said. "They aren't taking us to him, are they?"

"No. Gregor's cousin is alpha of a pack in Pennsylvania, and we're going to stay with them. They have a good life there, you'll see. We'll all be safe now." He seemed relieved beyond measure, so the others took him at his word and settled in for the drive. Most of the little ones went to sleep.

Frankie drove as quickly as he dared. They were pretty packed in, and his mind was on getting them all back to the pack as fast as he safely could.

"What happened?" Vladimir asked.

"One of the pups recognized Cheever, and Casimir had to take out the guards. There were only two of them. And then we got the others out of there."

"The tranquilizers didn't last as long as I thought they would, but they bought us enough time to make it back, though not much more."

Vladimir patted Frankie's leg. "Did the trip jog your memory?"

Frankie sighed and shook his head. "I've never been there before. None of it was familiar to me, and I still don't know why the guys were sent to find me." He tried not to be too disappointed and kept his attention on the road. What was important right now was getting all of them back to the pack compound safely. "Call your father so he knows that we're on our way back."

Vladimir nodded. "I'll try. Cell service there is really spotty."

Frankie had known that, but they were coming back with seven more wolves than they'd left with, much earlier than expected.

Vladimir didn't get through, but he left a message for his father, then turned to the others. "Do you think they're going to try to find us?"

"Yes," Cheever answered from the back. "Alpha Romeroff doesn't give up on anything unless he's forced to. And even then, he makes someone suffer. Monty and Patre, those two wolves, will try to follow us, because if they don't, there will be hell to pay. But they are going to have to go back and get vehicles first. And even though they don't know where we're going, the longer we're on this road, the more likely it is that they're going to find us."

"Is there an alternate route?" Frankie asked.

"Yes. Make a left turn about two miles ahead, and we'll take country roads. It will add miles to the trip, but it should also throw them off and make it less likely they'll be able to follow us." Cheever gave him the directions, and as the roads got worse, he was forced to slow down. He wasn't happy about that, but it couldn't be avoided.

"Go faster," Vladimir whispered.

"I can't. The road is bad, and it will bump everyone too much." He continued on, his anxiety growing by the second. He wished they had stayed on the main road and just made a break for it. But it was too late now.

About half an hour from the pack compound, they came to a main road, and Frankie made the turn, speeding up and heading for the compound while the others watched out the windows.

"There's truck coming up behind us fast," Cheever said. "Speed up if you can."

Frankie hit the gas, but the van was old and didn't have much power to begin with. He also didn't want to take the chance that the vehicle would become unstable. The truck grew closer in his mirror, and Frankie held his breath and let it pass.

They all released a breath as the truck disappeared ahead of them.

"How much longer?" one of the cubs asked. "My legs hurt, and I have to go potty."

The cry was echoed by the others.

"Maybe fifteen minutes," Frankie answered and picked up speed again.

FINALLY HE made it to the pack compound and parked the van. Everyone piled out and headed for the pack house, the pups making use of the woods as needed. They were quiet but sweet kids, and by the time they arrived at the main pack building, there was a huge welcome committee. Frankie met Martha, and she passed Victor to him. He held the baby, grateful that they were all safe. The little guy curled right against him, and he rocked him gently. Martha smiled as Victor closed his eyes.

"He remembers you," Martha told him with a gentle pat on the shoulder, gazing at him like he hung the moon. "You know it takes a strong person to do what's best for someone else."

Frankie shook his head. "I'm nothing special." Part of him missed the little guy, but Martha and Casimir adored the little pup. Frankie loved him too, but all he had to do was lift his gaze to the way Martha beamed at Victor to know that being with her was right for Victor. Martha would always adore him, and they were all pack. Victor would be happy, healthy, and loved—Frankie had no doubt of that.

Victor stretched and his thumb slipped between his lips, his eyes half closed.

"Yes, you are. You risked your own safety to rescue him and provide for him in the woods. And you nearly got yourself killed protecting him. True bravery is helping others, regardless of the cost to yourself." Frankie carefully passed Victor to Martha, who cradled him before taking him off to be fed.

Around him, Frankie found fathers embracing mates and pups, family units once broken and now brought back together. Haunted expressions had turned to those of quiet joy. "Where will we stay?" one of the women asked.

"We'll figure it out," Vladimir answered gently. "You're here and you're safe, and so are your pups. We'll all make room." Vladimir stepped away from the others, greeting his father and most likely explaining what happened.

"Everyone, come inside. There's food on the stove, and the rest of the pack will want to meet you." The alpha held open the door in welcome, and the others all filed quietly inside.

Frankie waited for Vladimir, sliding an arm around his waist as the two of them brought up the rear.

"I'm glad everything worked out," Vladimir told him softly. "Though I hated every second that you were away. I could feel you, though, and I knew you were okay. A few times I felt your fear and wanted to rush out to try to find you." He tugged Frankie closer. "Don't do that again."

"We did good, and things went pretty smoothly, all things considered." Even as he said the words, something nagged at the back of his mind. Frankie knew this wasn't the end, and the more he thought about it, the more he knew they needed to be prepared. "Your father's cousin knows where this pack is."

Vladimir nodded. "But he doesn't know we're involved."

Frankie shook his head. "Don't be so sure." Some notion pushed at the back of his mind, but he couldn't quite put his finger on it. "He isn't stupid, and if he wants these people back or wants to make those who helped them pay, their trail will lead him here."

Vladimir tugged him closer. "I know. I'm sure this is going to make him as angry as hell. But there was nothing else we could do."

They lifted their gazes to the new families sitting together, pups on fathers' laps, mates sitting so close to one another they could be one. Worry and joy mixed together in a weird olfactory stew, spiced with relief. All of these wolves had been under immense stress for a long time, and now, finally, they could relax. "We can't allow our brothers to be persecuted like this."

"I know. But what will we do when he comes for us?" Frankie asked. "You know he will." He didn't want anything to happen to any of them.

"We'll deal with that when it happens," Vladimir said.

Frankie knitted his eyebrows. "Huh? We can't just wait for him to show up." He shifted his weight from foot to foot.

"The alpha and the rest of the pack were talking about that while we were gone. They knew this was going to spark a conflict, but it couldn't be helped. The only good thing is that we're hundreds of miles away from his pack, and he's going to have to transport his people." Vladimir sighed. "Do you think he'll come himself?"

Frankie shrugged. He had no idea.

"We'll figure it out," Vladimir told him.

Frankie wished he could feel so confident. At least he was back with the pack, and hopefully things would be quiet for a little while anyway. And maybe he and his mate could have a little time to themselves.

CHAPTER 13

VLADIMIR WAITED until the others had eaten and the pack had found places for the new families to stay. Every building was full to bursting, but surprisingly, there were no fights. His father had easily made all the arrangements, and everyone was getting settled. He had put up two of the families in the pack house, the old place feeling like a home for the first time since Vladimir's mother had passed away. Now it was full of people all the time. Vladimir thought that might be good for his father. The alpha spent too much time alone.

Frankie yawned and sat back in one of the chairs, closing his eyes, the pup on his lap half asleep as well. The little boy's mother lifted him and carried him off to bed, and Vladimir tugged Frankie to his feet. "Come on, let's go. We've all had a very busy day."

Frankie nodded, and the two of them went to their cabin. "You know, I love being part of the pack. Those pups, they're so afraid all the time." He leaned on Vladimir as they made their way across the quiet compound. "Apparently the guards weren't subtle about what would happen to all of them if their fathers and mates failed to do what Alpha Romeroff wanted."

Frankie drew closer. "He seems to spread fear wherever he goes." He sighed.

"I know, and we're going to have to deal with him when the time comes." The crappy thing was that none of them had any idea when that would be. "Go on to the cabin. I'll be there as soon as I talk to my father." Vladimir was as tired as everyone else, but they were going to need a plan to protect the pack from this looming threat.

Frankie turned as soon as Vladimir pulled away. "I'm going with you. If we're going to figure this out, we need to do it together."

Vladimir was smart enough to know that he wasn't going to win this argument. Sighing, he went in search of his father. He found him down by the stream.

"Dad," Vladimir said as the last light of the day faded from the sky, turning the world dark purple and black. "We were looking for you."

He nodded in the near darkness. Fortunately Vladimir had good night vision. "I always come to this spot when I need to think. When I was a pup, this was where my father always found me when I disappeared." The water gurgled over the rocks. "I loved that sound. It helped clear my head." He had his hands behind his back as he faced the water. "I've been here for an hour, and I keep wondering when I'm going to figure out what to do. But I keep coming up empty."

"Dad, you know the pack is behind you," Vladimir said.

"Yes, and I'm trying to determine how to keep them safe." He turned toward the two of them. "I suppose you're here to find out what I plan to do?"

Vladimir shrugged. They knew that his father was still hurting because of Dimitri. How could he not?

"Actually, we came to try to help. We don't have any answers either. We're pretty sure your cousin is going to follow us here eventually, if for no other reason than to check to see if we were the ones behind the jail-break." Vladimir clenched his teeth, thinking of those poor women and children. "And he's going to want to put all of us in our places."

His father nodded. "I know."

"So what do we do?" Frankie asked.

"I already have some of the men patrolling the perimeter in case they show up. I doubt my cousin is going to try to sneak in; that isn't his style. He'll come in the front and try to intimidate us if he can. That's more his style. He likes to be the center of attention. Besides, his sneaky tactics have already failed, and he knows it."

"But what will we do?" Frankie asked.

"Nothing. When he comes, he's going to be coming for me. He and I are going to have to deal with this like wolves, and that means he'll challenge me. It's what he's always wanted. This is the pack that turned its back on him, and now he's going to return and try to conquer it."

"That can't happen," Vladimir gasped. "I won't have my family, my pack, torn apart like that. We deserve something better than to be ruled by a monster who would hold some of his pack members prisoner. That…." Vladimir turned back toward Frankie. He would not allow his mate to suffer under someone like that. He thought of Martha and Casimir, Sasha, little Victor, all the others in the pack…. No, he'd die before he let that happen.

"There comes a time in our lives when we all have to fight for what we want. I've done my best to protect this pack and keep us all safe. I've always hoped that living our lives here, away from others, where we could be close to the land and not bother anyone, would keep us safe. And it has… until recently."

"I'm sorry. I…," Frankie said.

The alpha turned to him. "This isn't your fault, Frankie. This is the outside world pushing in on us. I tried to stop it, but the outside world is more powerful. For whatever reason, you made your way here. Maybe you were drawn here because of your mate."

"I was blind. I had no idea where I was going. But I had to get away for Victor's sake." Frankie gasped. "Oh my God, I remember." Frankie held Victor's arm tightly. "The cloud… it's gone. I can remember."

"Why?" Vladimir asked. "I mean, what changed?"

Frankie shrugged. "I don't know. I think it's just the thought of Gregor coming here that's loosened the hold on my memory. I remember. I remember *everything*." He stared in the darkness. "Victor is my sister's child. After having Victor, she grew weaker and weaker and asked me to take care of Victor."

"Was your sister mated?" Vladimir asked.

"No, she wasn't. She said that Gregor was Victor's father but asked that if anything happened to her, I take him away. Lily didn't want Victor to be raised by that man." Frankie leaned harder against Vladimir.

"I'm sorry."

"But it's worse than that." Frankie sniffed slightly. "She told me that Gregor had taken her by force. That she hadn't wanted to be with him, but he had pressed himself on her." Frankie held him tightly. "She died when Frankie was about three months old, and I did as she asked. I took him away and tried to find a pack I had heard about down here." Frankie gasped as the grief must have welled inside him. "To think I forgot my own sister and everything she went through." He gasped again. "We can't let Gregor have any part of this pack. He'll destroy it. Matehood means nothing to him."

"It's okay," Vladimir said gently. He wished that Frankie hadn't had to go through all that.

"No, it's not. Gregor is ruthlessly selfish and power-hungry. If given the chance, he'll take over this pack, kill the leadership, and assimilate everyone else into what he considers his dominion, where no one is safe from anything he wants... anything. That's why I was holed up in that cave."

"You should have come to us," the alpha said.

"I know that now. But I had been told stories about the pack down here. I knew you were my only chance, and yet I remembered stories of how evil you were and that you wouldn't welcome outsiders." Frankie wiped his eyes, and Vladimir held him.

"Let me guess. They were Gregor's stories," Vladimir said.

"Yeah. But I didn't know what was real then. The car had run out of gas, and I was stuck. I feel bad about all of this. But at least I didn't hurt anyone—not intentionally."

"Who clouded your memory?" the alpha asked.

"I think, maybe, Dimitri did." It would have required the help of dark forces, but it was possible. Raisa had thought so, and Vladimir trusted her judgment.

The alpha stepped closer. "How could he? Dimitri said that you didn't see him."

"Yeah, but Frankie would have smelled him. I bet he learned that sort of thing from your cousin and he bound up Frankie's memories to confuse him. It would make it so much easier to take him out. And then, even if Frankie did survive, he wouldn't be able to remember anything and Dimitri would be safe."

"But the silver knife…."

"Dad, I don't know. We may never know exactly what motivated him."

Frankie approached Vladimir's father. "This wasn't something you did. Dimitri was influenced, but he ultimately made his own decisions. He decided that he wanted to lead the pack and was determined to take over. It's even possible that once he consolidated his power, he would see to it that you got moved out of the way." Frankie sighed. "Then I'm willing to bet your cousin would have moved in and either incorporated the pack with Dimitri's help, or simply taken it from him. Either way, Gregor would get what he wanted." He backed away, and Vladimir hugged his father.

"You've protected all of us for a long time. I see that now. I don't know how we're going to fight him off when he shows up, but we will. You, me, the betas, all of us. We will do it together. The pack is going to need to stand together against this threat. That's the only thing that can work against a wolf like Gregor."

"Yes," Frankie echoed. "It has to be all of us. We're stronger together than any of us is alone. You are the strongest among us, but this threat is one that will affect every single pack member. You don't have to bear this responsibility alone."

All of a sudden, the world seemed to turn on itself.

The area around them grew darker, and Vladimir clamped his eyes closed as brilliant light suddenly shone all around him. He gasped, wondering what was happening. Frankie stood next to him, holding his arm tightly. Slowly, Vladimir tried opening his eyes. "Where are we?"

"Where do you think?" a female voice asked. "You can see. My light will never hurt you."

To his surprise, Vladimir was able to open his eyes without issue, and he glanced around him.

Vladimir and Frankie stood alone in a wooded glade under trees with huge branches that reached toward the sky. A brook flowed nearby, light flashing off droplets of water. What was strange was that beyond the trees it was dark, like night was being held at bay right where they were standing. Small animals cavorted nearby, and birds flew around them.

"Vladimir, have we died and gone to Disney World?" Frankie asked.

A slightly rotund woman with a smile and cherry-red cheeks stepped out from behind the nearest tree. It took Vladimir a second to realize that she was the source of the light. She didn't glow or anything, but light seemed to radiate from her. It was strange and beautiful all at once. "Don't you know me, Vladimir?" the woman asked.

"Should I?" he asked, looking around as a sense of well-being and comfort filled him. Vladimir's breathing relaxed, and he blinked. "I do. You're the goddess, the mother of us all."

"Very good." She smiled again. "And I'm the one responsible for bringing you your mate. I knew you would make sure that Victor would be raised in love. That's the only way the darkness can be banished forever." She turned to Frankie. "Though I was beginning to despair that you would ever actually meet." She threw her hands in the air. "Even a goddess can only do so much. I thought I was going to have to call up a flood to get you out of that cave. Though that would have been preferable to what actually happened. But all's well that ends well." She winked. Vladimir had no idea if she was serious or not.

"We met and everything turned out, until it all went to hell," Vladimir said. "What are we supposed to do now? We did what was right. We helped those who needed it."

She raised her perfect eyebrows. "You do have a temper, don't you? Just like your father."

"Yeah, he does. And he's lusty too," Frankie teased. "So thanks for that."

"I like him," the goddess said to Vladimir. "He has a sense of humor."

"So do I, when something is funny." Vladimir needed to know why they were here and if she was going to help them with Gregor when he inevitably showed up.

She tapped her foot impatiently, and the ground vibrated under her feet. A few leaves fell from the tree. The animals scampered away to hide, and the birds flew up into the branches.

"Don't make her mad," Frankie whispered.

"Fine, I just don't like my life and my family being messed with. These are good people, and we work hard and look after one another. We pray to the goddess and steward her creations."

"Yes, you do. And I look after you. By the way, your miner friends are about to pack up and move away. What they seek is not for them to find." She stopped the tapping, and the world around them settled back down.

"What do you want from us?" Vladimir asked.

"Nothing. You and your mate have proven your-selves. You put your relationship and yourselves in dan-ger for others, and so I decided to reward you. Frankie, your memory was fully restored. I wish I could have done it sooner, but things like that are not always within my power. The magic was removed, and you are fully yourself once again." She glided closer, her white robe flowing around her like no fabric Vladimir had ever seen.

"Please… what do we do about Gregor?" Vladimir asked, looking into her surprisingly sad eyes. Maybe being a goddess wasn't all it was cracked up to be.

She shook her head. "I can't fight your battles for you. Gregor, your father's cousin, is someone out of my control. He is not able to see my light, so I can't touch him. But I can tell you that you and your mate are on the right track. Stick together, along with your pack, to protect each other and the one who wears my mark." She glided closer. "You're both just beginning to come into your potential. Vladimir as a leader and Frankie as one with a heart of gold and a spine of steel that he's just coming to understand that he possesses, though it's always been there. Work together—it's the best way to defeat those who have turned away from the light." She came closer and touched Vladimir's shoulder. "This battle has been waged for a very long time. It isn't going to be settled by you or your mate." She stepped back, and the scene around them began to fade. "Remember that all is not necessarily as it seems and that your rival is more than what you think."

"My rival?" Vladimir asked as night grew closer. "I don't understand."

"There was a reason that he wanted your mate re-turned. You need to figure that out and put an end to it."

Vladimir blinked as the light faded. The towering trees around them shortened, the branches transforming into the familiar forest and brook of their home. The glade around them dimmed as the normal world came back into focus.

The alpha turned to both of them. "How does this work?"

Vladimir blinked as he found himself once again standing in front of his father, who was talking as though nothing had happened. "This all standing together, how do you see this working? Wolves are a hierarchy with the strongest at the top."

Vladimir hesitated for a second, trying to reorient himself and digest the implications of the goddess's visit.

"True," Vladimir said, thinking quickly. His father had no idea what had just happened. Hell, he wondered if Frankie had actually been there or if the whole thing had been a figment of his imagination.

"It was real," a voice whispered on the wind and then faded away.

He turned to Frankie, who nodded, his eyes wide as though he was trying to figure out what had just happened as well.

Vladimir hugged his father just for entertaining the option. "I'm not sure, but maybe we can sleep on it and talk in the morning. Is that okay?" He had to support his father, and Vladimir wasn't going to demean his dad in any way. He had ideas, but they weren't formed yet, and he wanted to discuss them with his dad and get his input instead of railroading him. The goddess had said he was on the right track. And if that was true, he needed to formulate a plan right away.

"Thank you," his father said softly, then turned back to the water, and Vladimir gently guided Frankie away.

"Did what I think happened... just happen?" Frankie asked. "Did you and I find ourselves in the presence of the goddess herself?" Frankie spoke as though she might be listening. Maybe she was; Vladimir had no clue.

"Yes. And she doesn't appear to just anyone. We should be honored."

"So what do we do now?"

"She told us we were on the right path—that's something." Now all he needed to do was figure out how to find a way to save their pack while on that path. And what had the goddess said about Frankie and Gregor? He needed to figure out what that meant and what Gregor wanted... for both their sakes.

VLADIMIR CLOSED the door to their cabin and pressed Frankie back toward the bed. Frankie chuckled lightly as he held on. "I take it someone is ready to go." Frankie held him by the shoulders. "I need to see Victor."

Vladimir blinked and backed away, the words somehow sinking into his clouded mind. "Huh?"

"I need to see him. He's my sister's child, and I only now remembered that." He lowered his gaze. "And you heard what she said—that we were to protect the pack and the one that bears her mark. That must be Victor. Raisa saw the birthmark and wondered what it meant, and now we know. We have to protect him." He pushed away.

"How do you want to do that?" Vladimir asked as he adjusted his pants. His mind might be able to switch gears, but his body was another matter. He was ready for some alone time with his mate. "Martha and Casimir will take great care of him, and they already love him." If Frankie wanted, Vladimir would raise the pup with his mate. But as far as he was concerned, that was up to Frankie.

"They love him, and so do I. I had forgotten about my sister, and now I have all these feelings that were suppressed." He paused with his hand on the door. "Do you think that was why my memory was taken? If I didn't get close to Victor, then maybe I'd give him up if I were threatened?" Frankie paled.

"If that was the goal, then whoever put that spell on you failed. You would never do that. You placed Victor with two people who will bring up your sister's child with all the love in the world, and you are here. He will be raised with a committed couple, you, and the pack. What more could any pup ask for? Victor will know more love and care than any one of us could provide alone."

"I know that," Frankie said. "And I also know that taking Victor away from them would hurt two people I've come to care deeply about. I don't intend to do that. Martha will love and care for Victor in a way I could never. She will be his mother, the best stand-in for my sister that I could possibly find. Martha has a lot of my sister's steel in her spine. I just need to see him."

Frankie pulled the door open, and Vladimir followed him out of the cabin and across the compound. He knocked on the door, and Martha opened it.

"Is something wrong?" she asked, poised to pounce.

"Not immediately," Vladimir said gently, trying to diffuse her worry. "Frankie remembers everything now. It's a long story, and I'll explain what I can to both of you. But it seems that that Victor's birthmark is a gift from the goddess."

She stepped back and motioned them inside.

Casimir sat in a chair near the cold fireplace with Victor on his lap. The huge wolf appeared as gentle and paternal as Vladimir had ever see him. "Of course he is. This is the best pup ever." Casimir made light of Vladimir's comment. Not that he could blame him.

Frankie went over to Victor and gently placed his hand on his head. "What Vladimir said is serious. He has been marked by the goddess herself." Frankie knelt down, watching Victor sleep. "I should have known, but so many details were locked away."

Martha sat down in the chair near Casimir. "I think you need to explain what you mean. How do you know?"

"Because she told us… tonight." Frankie stood. "Victor's mother was my sister, and Alpha Romeroff is his father. He forced himself on my sister, and she got pregnant. She told me that if anything happened to her, I was to get Victor away from him. So that's what I did." Vladimir could feel Frankie's anxiety. "Anyway, tonight, not an hour ago, the goddess made her presence known to the two of us. She, in essence, told us to protect the one she had marked." He took a deep breath. "I just needed to see him. I honestly couldn't remember who this sweet little guy was until the goddess restored my memory." Frankie turned away, and Vladimir knelt next to him, holding Frankie tightly.

"Do you want to take him with you?" Martha asked, fear running off her.

"Yes, I do. But I'm not going to." Frankie stood, wiping his eyes. "You and Casimir have grown close to him. I was just telling Vladimir that you remind me of my sister, and I would be honored if...." Frankie sniffed again. "I...." He took another deep breath and held it. "I want to do what's best for Victor, and him being with you, raised by the pack with love, is what I think is best." Frankie stood with a soft sigh.

"Do you want to hold him?" Casimir asked. Frankie nodded, so Casimir stood and gently shifted Victor to Frankie, where he easily settled in his arms.

"Thank you." Frankie gazed at his nephew, and Vladimir realized that Frankie was grieving for his sister and that loss, as well as trying to establish a connection with Victor himself. Vladimir could feel his mate's confusion and pain.

Victor stretched and opened his eyes, staring up at both of them. He reached for Frankie and gripped one of Frankie's fingers. "You're going to be a great one. You know that? The goddess has touched you, and all of us will love you and keep you safe."

Victor opened his little mouth and wrinkled up his face, clearly getting ready to cry for a feeding. Frankie passed him to Martha, who had a bottle ready. "Thank you."

"No, sweetheart," Martha said gently. "We need to thank you. This little one has brought something into our lives that we never thought we could have." She leaned forward and kissed Frankie on the cheek.

Some of Frankie's anxiety seemed to slip away, and he nodded and then looked toward the door. "We should go." He left the cabin, and when Vladimir closed the door behind him, Frankie turned to him with a slight smile. "He's going to be okay. I think we all are."

Vladimir hoped he knew what he was talking about.

THE TWO of them walked across the compound, pausing in the clearing to look up at the stars. It was a quiet night, and Vladimir moved up behind Frankie, winding his arms around his waist. "Sometimes you blow me away with how caring and thoughtful you are."

Frankie leaned back against him, humming softly as they stood together, the sounds of the night echoing around them. After maybe half an hour, Frankie took his hand and slowly moved away, tugging Vladimir into their cabin. As soon as the door clicked closed, Vladimir hefted Frankie into his arms and propelled them both toward the bed.

"I need to make sure you're okay. I watched you disappear into the woods and then return again. My wolf needs to check you over, and he isn't going to wait any longer." Vladimir tugged off Frankie's shirt, running his fingers over his skin, loving the hum of soft pleasure that rang in Frankie's throat.

"Where are the pups?" Frankie breathed.

Vladimir growled and hurried over to pull open the door. He whistled, and the pups came bounding inside. Vladimir closed the door and flashed them his wolfy teeth, and they immediately settled on their blanket on the floor. "Good pups," Vladimir soothed before stalking back to this mate.

He pulled Frankie's pants off before stripping and climbing onto the small bed. He never would have thought that it was big enough for two, but he and Frankie tended to sleep curled together, so the bed worked for them. Still, tonight, it seemed small, and Vladimir ended up tugging the bedding onto the floor, lifting Frankie down, and laying him out on the blankets.

"Isn't this a little much?"

"I want to see you," he growled and bent closer, his gaze raking over Frankie's body. "Damn, you're gorgeous, and perfect for me." He leaned closer, inhaling deeply, taking in Frankie's slightly sweet, intoxicating scent. "I could smell you forever, and you taste—" He ran his tongue up Frankie's belly. "—like ambrosia, the food of the gods." His entire body quivered at seeing Frankie laid out, waiting. This was his mate, the one person meant only for him, and as far as Vladimir was concerned, the goddess had smiled down on him in a huge way. Vladimir would forever thank her for his Frankie.

"I want you. All I could think about as we were running back to the van was, what if something happened and I didn't make it back? I had a child in my arms, but I could feel you in my heart, calling to me, and all I wanted was to get back to you because then I'd know I was safe." Frankie tugged him down into a deep kiss. Vladimir's hands continued to roam, feeling every inch of his mate, assuring his wolf that no harm had come to his beloved.

"I need to mark you again," Vladimir said as instinct and the need to make Frankie his once more overwhelmed him.

"Oh goddess, yes," Frankie groaned as Vladimir sank down on his mate's body, sucking a trail along his sweet skin. His mate's moans and whimpers, the muscles quivering under his hand—all fueled his passion.

Vladimir's wolf wasn't going to be denied for long, and driven by instinct, he slowly entered Frankie and groaned. "Damn, you're perfect for me." He held Frankie, their merged bodies going wild even without any movement. This was perfection. Being with his mate was the greatest thing he'd ever experienced, and Vladimir would give his life to keep him happy.

"You too... now move," Frankie growled, pushing against him. Damn, Frankie was horny and demanding. Vladimir loved it. He rolled his hips, filling Frankie and driving his senses wild as the scents of arousal, sweat, and passion hung heavily in the air. He inhaled deeply, surrounded by the smell of his mate as he took what he needed, blown away at how readily Frankie gave to him. "More...," Frankie breathed.

"I don't want to hurt you." Vladimir's wolf pushed to the surface, and it took all his willpower to keep the shift from coming over him. His wolf wanted his mate and wasn't going to wait any longer. Vladimir closed his eyes, pushing the wolf back even as he picked up the pace in order to give his wolf what he wanted.

Frankie shook under him, gripping Vladimir's arms tightly, pressing against him.

Skin slapped skin, and moans filled the room. "Please...."

Damn, Frankie begging for him, wanting him, was so very, very sexy. Vladimir gave himself over to the passion, and his mate cried out, adding their passion to the sultry air.

"I'm not gonna last...." Frankie's words worked some sort of magic on Vladimir, and his own release pushed from deep inside him, welling upward. Just before it crashed into him, he struck, sending both of them barreling off the cliff into their own cataclysmic releases.

CHAPTER 14

THE NEXT two days were really busy for them all. The pack leadership met to devise a strategy for handling any impending threats, and then they opened the session to the entire pack. The three new families really seemed to fit in, though it was too soon to determine if that would last. It was clear that the young ones got along famously, melding into the various groups of pups. Still, an air of tension ran through everyone.

Frankie spent the days working on the new cabin, which he and Vladimir had decided would be for one of the new families. The newcomers needed the space more than the two of them did. Frankie liked their little cabin. It was theirs and cozy, and he had a pretty good idea that in the wintertime, it would be toasty warm, where a larger space would be more difficult to heat.

"I hate this waiting," Frankie told Vladimir as they hoisted one of the newly dressed logs into place for the outside cabin walls.

"There's nothing we can do," Vladimir said. "We just have to be prepared and hope the threat never comes." They lowered the log into place and prepared to hoist the ones for the corresponding side walls so they could verify notches before making final cuts.

A large form stepped out from the trees.

"Ruck," Frankie said happily. "Did you come to help?" Their bear friend had taken to stopping by more often after Vladimir told him about the threat they expected.

Ruck's expression darkened, and as soon as the log was checked, Frankie and Vladimir lowered it back to the ground, and they approached their friend. "What is it?"

"The miners are leaving. They're giving up," he reported.

"That's good." The stream and the woods would be much better off without them.

Ruck nodded. "But there are strangers in the woods—wolves. I saw them about three miles north. They were on foot, heading in this direction. Maybe four or five of them. And they're big. They mean business."

"Thank you," Vladimir said. "I figured it was only a matter of time."

Vladimir's father joined them, and Vladimir filled him in. "We appreciate you warning us," the alpha said.

Frankie didn't expect Ruck to stay. This wasn't his fight, and he had learned enough about bears and their solitary nature to know that he was probably being as helpful as he could.

Ruck nodded to the alpha and then turned and disappeared back into the woods. Vladimir's father turned and called out to his pack, "Get the pups and young ones into the pack house with their mothers. The rest of you, stow your tools and work and take up positions. Call as soon as you see anyone."

Vladimir was proud of his pack. No one raised their voice or panicked.

"Martha," Vladimir said, stopping her. "I know you want to stand with your mate and the rest of us, but I have a job for you." She paused, listening, so he continued. "If things start to go bad, we need you to grab a car and get everyone out of here. I know it will hurt, but the pack needs to be safe. Those of us who are fighting need to know that our families aren't going to fall under Gregor's thumb."

"But they'll probably have people watching the pack house."

Vladimir shook his head. "They have no idea that we know how many there are. We'll just make sure that all of them are in the compound. Just tell everyone to be quiet and go out the door on the other side. Don't look back or worry about us. We will meet you at the ice cream parlor in Eagles Mere once it's all over. I hope this won't be necessary, but we can't take any chances. Will you do this?"

Martha nodded. "You can count on me." She turned and guided the others into the pack house, then closed the doors.

The pups ran circles around Vladimir's feet, and he thought of sending them inside, but there was no sense. If the others needed to get away, they were going to have to go quickly. He'd already asked Raisa to take the pups with her.

"Let's get back to work," Vladimir told the men and received confused looks. "At least look like you're working. And Frankie, stay out of sight." He wanted to tell him to go into the pack house with the others, but he knew his mate wouldn't consider it.

"Well, well," a strange, deep voice called, and Vladimir turned as a huge wolf stepped out of the woods, followed by three others. "Little Frankie." He smiled, but his eyes were dark as coal.

"What are you doing here, Gregor?" Alpha Corelia asked. "You were turned out of this pack years ago and aren't welcome here."

Gregor puffed out his chest, crossing his arms. "I came for what's mine. Frankie, these three and their families, and… my son."

Vladimir had to give his father credit—he didn't flinch. "There is no one here that belongs to your or your pack. Frankie is mated and has decided to settle here, as have the other families. They are part of my pack now, of their own free will. You have no further claim on any of them." Damn, his father was impressive.

Frankie stood next to Vladimir, holding himself erect. Vladimir was so damned proud of his mate. Frankie might have been afraid, but he didn't show it in any way. That was inspiring.

"You don't get to decide that, cousin," Gregor growled as he stepped forward. He was half a head taller than Vladimir's father, huge, strong, and oozing power and Dirk Greysonity. "I can do what I want and take what I want. You may have been able to stop me when I was younger, but you can't now." As he stared at the alpha, the others moved closer.

"Oh, but you're wrong. I do get to decide." His father smiled. "By the way, you might want to call out your other man, the one sneaking through the woods." Vladimir saw the enemy alpha's jaw clench. This was their territory. Did Gregor think his father wouldn't know there was someone else? "If you decide to press your case, you're going to need him."

"I don't think so," Gregor laughed as Sasha, Casimir, and Cheever struck, pressing knives to the backs of all three of Gregor's men.

"I think so. The knives are silver, just like the one you gave to my son." The alpha narrowed his gaze. "Did you think I wouldn't know what you'd done, that I wouldn't get to the bottom of it?" His father didn't break his gaze from Gregor's as the fifth wolf made an appearance from around the side of the pack house. "I suggest you tell your man to back off or all three wolves will get a lethal dose of silver. Those knives have been enhanced and roughed up. If they go in, I can guarantee that bits of the silver will stay inside them, poisoning their blood, and that will be their end." That was one of the most dangerous parts of the plan they had come up with, but Vladimir had been sure that Gregor would come with muscle that they would need to neutralize.

"Stand down," Gregor called from between clenched teeth as his eyes practically glowed in anger. "Your son…," Gregor spat. "Your son. You're the one without a clue. Dimitri does not carry your blood. He's my son, and I want to see him now. What did you do to him?" The huge alpha shook with anger, and Vladimir knees weakened slightly at the revelation. God, that explained so much. It was still a shock to know that… wait….

"How is that possible… unless…?" Vladimir said.

Gregor glanced toward him. "I see you've worked it out."

Vladimir felt himself paling. "You forced yourself on my mother the same way you did on Frankie's sister, didn't you?" He wanted this man dead in the worst way.

He knew his mother and father had loved each other deeply. What a horrible secret she'd had to keep.

Gregor answered with an evil smile. "It's an alpha's job to spread his essence as far as possible to ensure the next generation is as strong as possible. I took Frankie into my family just like I did his sister, but look how he betrayed me. No one walks away after taking what's mine." He bared his teeth, trying to intimidate the group, but Vladimir was too angry to care. Damn, his mate was a bigger hero than he knew for getting Victor away from this sociopath. Gregor might be strong, but he was pure evil.

"You hurt my mate." His father's words were measured, but he seethed with anger. Vladimir could see it in his rigid stance, and its dark, heavy scent permeated the air. "I'll kill you for that one day, just like I had to kill my… *your* son when he challenged me."

Now it was Gregor's turn to be shocked. He clenched his fists and lifted his head to the sky, howling in a booming voice that shook the air.

"I suggest you leave now. There is nothing for you here," Alpha Corelia said. Vladimir figured that wasn't totally true. If Victor was Gregor's son, then him finding out about Dimitri would only make him even more determined to get his hands on the little boy.

"Not without what I came for." Gregor stood taller, shaking off his anger. "Alpha Corelia, I—"

"You don't want to do that," Vladimir called loudly, interrupting the other alpha. This was the moment he had been planning for. He just hoped the ploy would work. Gregor was about to offer a challenge to his father, and Vladimir did not intend to allow that to happen.

"It is my right—" Gregor boomed, his voice filling the compound.

"Yes, it is. But if you challenge my alpha and you win, then I will be forced to challenge you," Vladimir said. "And while I'm not as big as you are, you will be weakened, and you have to answer the challenge immediately.

"Then me," Cheever called. Vladimir kept his gaze glued on Gregor as the implication sank in.

"And me," Sasha said.

"Then me," Casimir spoke up.

"Me too. We all will," another of the men added.

Ruck stepped out of the woods, bigger than any of the others. "I'll challenge you as well." He crossed his arms over his huge chest, eyes blazing with hate.

"We'll wear you down, one after the other, until you're too weak to move. Then we'll chop what is left of you into small pieces and scatter them in the woods so the foragers can feast on what's left of you. There will be no burial and no dignified ending. Then, once we're done and you and your men are gone, we'll take over your pack and give all those who deserve it sanctuary. The others we'll turn loose to fend for themselves, packless and alone." It was time to bring this to an end. He still wasn't sure his gamble was going to work, but he was prepared to do what he said he would.

"You aren't going to get any of us," Frankie yelled. "All of us, the entire pack, we stand together. You challenge one, you challenge all. And we will make you pay."

Gregor seemed to recover. "Why would you all put your lives at risk? I'm stronger than any of you, and I can rip you apart."

"That may be, but you aren't stronger than all of us together." Frankie stood tall next to him, and Vladimir nearly burst with pride at his mate. "No one has ever stood up to you. Well, we are. All of us, together. It may cost us dearly, but in the end, you will be gone, and we will rebuild a better world because you won't be in it." Frankie held Vladimir's arm. "I know what it's like to live under your cruelty and your brand of leadership. I would rather die than live that way again."

"We all would," Cheever boomed. "Now go."

Vladimir could see Gregor's indecision in his eyes.

"It's time for you to leave," Vladimir's father added. "You will get nothing here but misery and hurt. We will all see to that." He stepped forward. "Is it worth it, cousin? What do you have to gain? You can try to release your anger and greed on us, but you will pay for it with your life and those of your men." Vladimir knew his father was holding himself strong even though he was hurting deeply… as was Vladimir. But there was time for dealing with pain and hurt later. The threat to all of them had to be removed.

Vladimir could almost see the indecision behind Gregor's dark eyes. "You know this isn't over," he growled at Vladimir's father.

"Yes, it is. You need to go home and leave us all alone. Remember that we stand together, and you can't defeat that. Your own pack members don't care for you—most are desperate to get away. You don't lead, you dominate, and that leads to unhappiness and discontent." Vladimir's father held himself high. Vladimir and Frankie moved to stand next to him. "You can't win here. Not now, not ever. Go home."

Gregor took a single step back and then another before turning toward the trees. The others lowered their weapons but kept them nearby as the huge wolves moved to follow. "You may have won today...."

"Just go and don't come back."

Gregor and his men entered the woods, but Vladimir stayed on alert in case they tried something else. The area around them was almost unearthly quiet as they waited, no sounds of birds or animals in the air. Even the insects seemed to hold their breath and stop flying, waiting for what came next.

Vladimir dodged as a glint caught the sun. He tugged Frankie along with him, but his mate lunged and fell against him. They barreled into his father, the three of them falling to the ground in a heap. Vladimir had known deep down that Gregor wasn't about to leave without one parting shot.

"Are you both okay?" Vladimir asked, looking Frankie over as his father got back to his feet.

"I'm fine," his father said just as Vladimir saw the throwing knife, silver and deadly, embedded in Frankie's side. Frankie had taken the knife intended for him.

"Get Raisa!" the alpha shouted.

Vladimir barely heard the words as he crouched over his wounded mate. He pulled the knife free and dropped it to the dirt. "Sweetheart, you need to fight this," Vladimir said, hoping Frankie could hear him. His skin was pale and his eyes were closed. Vladimir put his ear to his chest. He was barely breathing.

"Vladimir," Raisa said as she crouched down with him, "let me look at him."

"You need to fight," Vladimir whispered to Frankie as he gave her room without letting go of him. The wound was still bleeding, the flow not slowing. "The knife is gone; you need to heal." He lifted his gaze to Raisa. "Why isn't he healing?"

"Probably because his body couldn't take any more silver." She put pressure on the wound and held it there, but Vladimir knew that he was losing his brave, selfless mate. The connection between them seemed to be fading, and Vladimir had no idea what to do. "It is in the hands of the goddess."

Vladimir latched on to Raisa's words and closed his eyes, trying to connect with the deity in some way. "Please help us." The thought of losing his mate ripped at his very soul. "You just brought us together. Please don't let him go."

"There is only so much I can do," a light voice said on the wind. Vladimir knew it was her.

"I'll do anything, just help us. Take me instead of him," Vladimir answered. He had no idea if the others could hear the voice. "My life is worthless without him." Vladimir clamped his eyes closed, praying, willing some of his strength into Frankie. It was his last hope.

Raisa moved next to him. "The bleeding has stopped," she said. "He's still breathing."

Vladimir didn't dare stop whatever he was doing. If it was working, he needed to send more—everything he had—to Frankie, to his mate, his love. "Please, Frankie, be strong."

"Rest now," the voice on the wind told him. "You've done all you can."

Fatigue overcame him like a wave he had no control over. Vladimir slumped onto the ground, his eyes closing, blackness surrounding him.

"WHERE'S FRANKIE?" Vladimir said as soon as he opened his eyes. He was back in his cabin, on his bed. "Where is he? What happened to him?"

Martha sat next to the bed with Victor in her arms. "He's up at the pack house. Raisa is watching over him. He was carried up there after you passed out. We brought you here." She patted his shoulder.

"Is he dead?" Vladimir asked.

"No. He was healing. The bleeding had stopped and his color was returning. I think he's going to be okay."

Vladimir pushed away the blanket and sat up, the room spinning. He closed his eyes and groaned, waiting for it to stop. "How long have I been here?" His stomach groaned angrily.

"Since yesterday. Whatever you did to save your mate was impressive. None of us has ever seen anything like that. You both must be favored by the goddess. That's the only explanation any of us can come up with."

Vladimir didn't move, waiting for his head to clear. "Did you hear her?" he asked, gingerly getting to his feet.

"Hear what? When?" Martha asked as Victor stretched without opening his eyes, his little lips pursing like he was looking for food. The stinker was probably going to wake up hungry any time. "I was inside, keeping the others calm. Why?"

"Never mind," Vladimir said, holding his head. Maybe it had all been a dream of some sort. His head wasn't functioning fully, and he needed to see Frankie. Vladimir thanked Martha and hurried out of the cabin, heading toward the pack house, where most of the pack was gathered, talking quietly. As soon as he came in, all conversation stopped. Parents gaped, and even the pups look at him as though he were strange. "Where's Frankie?"

"In here, son," his father told him.

Vladimir hurried into a room where Frankie lay on a bed, his eyes closed but his skin pink and his breathing normal.

"He's going to be fine. We've let him sleep, but he'll be ravenous when he wakes up, as I suspect you are."

Vladimir agreed with that. His belly rumbled once again.

"Go on and sit with him. I'll have someone bring in something for both of you to eat." His father didn't come near him. Instead, he actually hurried out of the room.

"Dad," Vladimir said, and his father paused just outside the doorway. "What's going on?"

"We heard her…. She was talking to you." His dad grew pale. "The goddess, she was talking… we all heard her." He lowered his gaze, and Vladimir half expected him to bare his neck.

"Don't…," Vladimir said gently. "Don't act that way."

"But the goddess was speaking to you. She's blessed you and your mate. I can't compete with that." He swallowed hard. "She granted what you asked."

"Yes, she did, Dad. I prayed, and she answered. But that doesn't change anything. You are still the leader of this pack, and I haven't changed my mind about that." He approached his father. "I do not want to be the alpha. I didn't do what I did to support you as some back door to take your position. And just so you know, the one blessed by the goddess is Victor… and this entire pack."

Frankie groaned behind him, and Vladimir went to him. "Hey, sleepyhead."

"What happened?" Frankie opened those incredible blue eyes, and Vladimir gently gathered him into his arms.

"I almost lost you," Vladimir said, inhaling deeply, needing to know his mate was whole and smelled the same, felt the same. Hell, he wanted to strip him naked, lick him all over, and inspect every inch of him to make sure he truly was okay, but that would probably have to wait until later. "There was a knife meant for me, and you took it."

A knock sounded on the door frame, and to Vladimir's shock, Ruck stepped inside. He said nothing but placed Gregor's black stone necklace on the table. Vladimir nodded and smiled. "Thank you, my friend." It was truly over.

"You and your mate are welcome," Ruck said and left the room.

"What did he bring?" Frankie asked.

"A souvenir of sorts. I didn't see who threw the knife, but it seems Ruck did, and he made sure that Gregor paid the ultimate price." He helped Frankie to his feet, and they left the room.

"How long have I been out?" Frankie asked.

"A day." He guided him out and to the table, where Martha rerouted the plates that had been prepared and set one in front of each of them. Frankie dug in as though he were famished. Vladimir did the same.

"Where did Ruck go?" Frankie asked.

"Your friend left right after he saw you. We tried to be nice to him, but he didn't seem entirely comfortable," Martha said as she sat down with Victor. "We'll be on the lookout for him and make sure he knows he's *always* welcome. It's probably a bear thing."

Vladimir hoped she was right.

"Why is everyone watching us?" Frankie whispered, glancing around once they had eaten some. "What did we do?"

Vladimir sighed and set down his fork. "Everyone, enough."

"But we heard her," Sasha said. "The goddess spoke to you."

"Yes, she did. And she helped me save my mate. I prayed, and she answered."

"So you are blessed," Sasha added. "I told you that's what it meant. We need to follow him and—"

"Stop," Vladimir said. "You need to do nothing." He turned in his seat. "The goddess spoke to me and Frankie. She guided the two of us and helped us rid our world of Gregor, but we are all blessed—the whole pack is. Not just him and me, but each and every one of us including Ruck. We all stood together, and it worked. That's what's important. I'm not your alpha. My father was and still is. He has led this pack for two decades, and he will continue to lead us into the future." Vladimir did his best to glare at all of them. "I don't want to be alpha. Nothing has changed... except that I found my mate, a gift from the goddess, and I thank her for that... again." He turned back to the table as the room erupted in conversation.

"You know they aren't going to believe you. Goddesses don't talk to just anyone," Frankie whispered to him. "You can say what you like, but they are going to form their own opinions."

Vladimir shook his head. "Then maybe you and I can live a quiet life and everything will return to normal." God, he wanted that more than anything, but Vladimir wasn't stupid. The pack's view of him had changed and their life was going to be different. Vladimir had no doubt about that.

For the time being, they were safe and the threat had been neutralized. That was all they could ask for. And now they all knew to be on their guard, which was a step forward.

Frankie shrugged and went back to eating. Yeah, they both knew he was deluding himself. Life was never going to be the same. Vladimir's brother was gone. Well, the traitor he'd always thought was his brother was dead. That was a lot to take in. His father had had part of his world ripped out from under him. The pack had grown significantly, and there would always be some sort of threat. And then there was this whole "blessed by the goddess" thing. Who knew what that was going to mean for Victor?

Vladimir's head swam, and he tried his best to process everything. He turned to the rest of the pack. "I mean it. Knock it off!" Half of them were still staring.

"You know, that sounded really alpha." Frankie bit his lower lip before laughing.

"You…." Vladimir tried to sound angry and failed.

"Vladimir," Sasha's youngest pup said as he slowly approached. Simon was four and usually full of energy. "Do you talk to the goddess all the time? 'Cause if you do, can you ask her where my red ball is? I can't find it. Maybe she knows." He was so earnest.

"The goddess doesn't talk to me all the time, but the next time she decides to visit, I'll ask her." What the hell else was he supposed to say?

Simon turned around and went back to his mom and dad.

"She doesn't know where it is either," Simon reported and rejoined the pups playing on the floor. Vladimir turned away before he completely lost it. Pups. They were something else. And speaking of pups, he looked around for the four wolves.

"They're outside," his father told him. "They're wild, and it's best if that's where they stay. The pack will make sure they have a place and a den, but other than that, they are going to need to start making their own way. All four of them are going to want to find mates of their own eventually." He sighed. "Maybe we should look at taking them back up to Canada when they're older so they can have a chance at having a family."

Vladimir nodded, but Frankie put a hand on his shoulder. "I was thinking the same sort of thing. But what if we brought down some wolves instead?" He grinned. "We could cross the border as wolves, locate a pack, and see if there are any members who would be willing to come join us here." It was something Vladimir had never thought about. "There would be another benefit. If there was a pack of wolves in the vicinity, it would give us a group to hide among. The humans would be baffled by it, but that hardly matters." He cocked his eyebrows, and Vladimir nodded.

"Let's think about it," the alpha said before sitting down across from them. Others joined, and soon some of the goddess reverence seemed to dissipate as everyone crowded around the table.

"What do we do now?" Casimir asked the alpha.

At first, most eyes traveled to Vladimir, which made him uncomfortable. Fortunately, his father answered. "We'll grieve for what we lost, celebrate the families we've gained, and figure out how to finish the housing we need to get all of us through the winter. We're going to have to organize hunting parties to ensure we have enough food… and we'll go on." He sat tall and straight, which was good to see. Vladimir knew his father was hurting deeply on the inside, but he didn't show it. That was what the pack needed right now. Strength and calm from their leader, and that was his father.

"Then let's get to work," Casimir said. "Everyone should meet at the building site. We have tasks for everyone who is able to help."

"Then Vladimir and I need to get busy," Frankie declared, and both of them stood and headed outside.

It was surprising what the pack could accomplish when they all worked together. One team got the logs prepped, and another set them in place. The cabin rose to the roofline, and then the first trusses to support the roof were constructed. It was an amazing sight, and by the end of the day, Vladimir was worn out, Frankie looked completely done in, and even the pups hung their heads a little low after spending the afternoon bringing them sticks, their contribution to the effort.

"We have dinner," Raisa said as she approached the group. "You've all worked enough. Come and eat."

The pack ate together in a cacophony of overlapping conversations, which was exactly as it should be. Once everyone had eaten, the pack gathered and took turns telling stories, with everyone wanting to know what the goddess was like.

"She's pretty, like the mother of all of us," Vladimir said.

"But she has a temper," Frankie said, and he told them about her tapping her foot and the ground rumbling. "Vladimir pissed her off. Does that sound familiar?" They all chuckled as Vladimir's father rolled his eyes and nodded. "Leaves fell and all the animals hid." His mate was having a good time. "But she smiled at me." He actually preened, and the others laughed. Vladimir didn't mind. His mate was happy, and that was all that counted.

"I THOUGHT you were tired," Frankie teased once they were in their cabin and Vladimir had stripped Frankie down and pressed him onto the mattress.

"I'm never too tired for you." And his wolf wanted his mate. It was that simple. "And I'll never grow tired of you." Vladimir held his mate to him, both of them naked, together in the most basic way. "You are my heart, and I will do anything for you."

Frankie swatted him on the butt. "I love you too."

"But don't you dare put yourself in danger like that again." Vladimir could still see the knife embedded in Frankie's side—a knife meant for Vladimir.

"Hey... I did it to save you," Frankie said. "I had to. I love you more than life itself."

Vladimir sighed. "I guess you proved that." Then he chuckled, his voice growing deeper. "But I can prove a great deal more." He silenced Frankie with a kiss and spent the next couple of hours proving just how much he loved his mate.

EPILOGUE

A FIRE blazed in the middle of the pack compound, throwing dancing light onto the surrounding cabins and pack house. "Is it time yet?" Simon asked as he stood with his parents, barely able to contain himself.

"In a few minutes," Simon's father said, placing a hand on his son's shoulder, his mate standing next to him as the pack all gathered. Tables had been set up just outside the pack house, and they groaned under the weight of venison, salmon, trout, and rabbit, as well as a number of other dishes. But it was the meat that had their mouths watering and stomachs rumbling.

Frankie joined Vladimir in front of their cabin as the last of the pack arrived.

Vladimir built up the fire until the flames leapt to the sky, and everyone grew quiet. Vladimir's father, their alpha, their leader, stepped into the circle, standing tall. The past month had been very difficult for him. But Vladimir had supported his father and filled some of the gaps while the alpha grieved for Dimitri, as well as what had happened to his mate all those years ago. Alpha Corelia was stronger and now stood taller than he had in a long time. And while Frankie and Vladimir knew of his difficulties, the rest of the pack didn't.

Vladimir had run interference for him so the pack would function properly.

The entire pack grew quiet, and even the wolf pups all sat right in front of him, paying attention to their alpha, giving him the respect he deserved.

"Pack mates, family, I want to welcome all of you to our full moon celebration. The past few months have been difficult for all of us. But those bumps in the road are nothing compared to what we can accomplish together. This is a celebration!" He lifted his head and howled into the night, everyone else joining in, including the pups. "Our pack continues to grow, and we welcome new members. Please step forward."

The three families from up north stepped forward. Where they had looked haggard and worried just weeks ago, now they were happy and healthy. It was a joy to see, and Frankie squeezed Vladimir's hand. Then he stepped forward, tugging Vladimir along with him.

"Not us," Vladimir said.

"Yes. You and your mate," Alpha Corelia said. "This is a celebration, and the claiming and accepting of your mate, and the blessings of the goddess, are cause for celebration as well." He grinned and then raised his hands to his mouth, sending out a deep howl into the woods. A minute later, Ruck stepped into the circle.

"Ruck, we all know you aren't a wolf, but we thought it important to include you tonight. Bears and wolves are different, we all know that, but we wanted you to know that you are welcome here. You've shown that you are part of our family, so for tonight—and anytime you wish—please join us. You are pack."

Frankie swallowed hard as Vladimir squeezed his hand. The change in the alpha didn't go unnoticed by anyone.

Vladimir's father approached each family and spoke to each individual, sniffing them, rubbing against them, transferring scent, making them officially pack. He went down the line, paying attention to each member. "Do you pledge your loyalty to this pack and to your brothers and sisters?"

"We do!" echoed through the clearing.

"Do you accept those pledges?"

"We do," the others echoed.

The alpha stepped back. "Then I declare us one pack, one family, one community, to provide and care for each other."

The entire pack lifted their heads and sent the cry of unity into the night.

"I wonder if she heard us?" Frankie whispered to Vladimir.

"I heard all of you," came a gentle voice on the breeze that wound through the group, touching each of them before falling away.

The alpha approached him and Vladimir, stepping close. He didn't say anything but slid his hand around the back of Vladimir's neck, bringing them close. Then he did the same with Frankie, looking deep into his eyes, smiling. With Ruck, he shook his hand, grinning.

"Can we eat now?" Simon asked.

"Yes, we can eat," the alpha said, motioning to the tables. And the feast was on.

Everyone lined up and took their turn filling plates, then sat around the fire. Frankie filled two plates and brought one for his mate, and they sat down beside each other. They didn't talk a lot, just ate and leaned against one another, the sense of contentment between them building into something more as their meal continued.

Once they had eaten and the stories began, Vladimir quietly excused himself, only to return a few minutes later. He took Frankie by the hand and, without a word, led him away from the fire and off toward the trees.

"Where are we going?" Frankie asked, able to see well enough to traverse the forest until the babble of the stream grew louder.

"This is one of my favorite places at night," Vladimir said as he spread out a blanket he'd hidden behind one of the trees. Then he guided Frankie down onto it and the two of them looked up through a clearing in the trees to millions of stars. "This is my place—now our place." He didn't move, and Frankie stared upward until the stars seemed to draw closer, cocooning them in their twinkling light. "I used to wonder what it would be like to make love under the stars."

Frankie hummed softly. "Then why don't we find out?" He rolled onto his side, tugging Vladimir close, and the two of them did just that.

DIRK GREYSON is very much an outside kind of man. He loves travel and seeing new things. Dirk worked in corporate America for way too long and now spends his days writing, gardening, and taking care of the home he shares with his partner of more than two decades. He has a master's degree and all the other accessories that go with a corporate job. But he is most proud of the stories he tells and the life he's built. Dirk lives in Pennsylvania in a century-old home and is blessed with an amazing circle of friends.

Facebook:www.facebook.com/dirkgreyson
Email:dirkgreyson@comcast.net

PREY FOR
LOVE

Best-Selling Author
DIRK GREYSON

The last three guys Phillip dated are dead. Is he next?

When successful businessman Phillip Barone attends a lover's funeral and discovers he was just the latest of Phillip's partners to die, Phillip knows he's in trouble.

He also knows just the man he needs.

Former Marine Barry Malone would love a second chance with Phillip—he just wishes the romance could be rekindled under better circumstances. But Phillip's stalker is escalating, and if Barry cannot solve the mystery of who wants Phillip dead and why, he might lose him for good. Barry's determined, but the investigation struggles against the wit of a crafty killer—one who is closer to Phillip than they could have realized.

Luckily Barry is even closer, and he'll do whatever it takes to protect the man he's falling in love with all over again.

www.dreamspinnerpress.com

DIRK
GREYSON

HELL AND BACK

Seventeen years ago, Forge Reynolds fell in love… and had his heart broken. When Staff Sergeant Gage Livingston was brought into Forge's Army field hospital, temporarily paralyzed, Forge sat with him, read his letters, answered his mail, and formed a connection he thought would last. But Gage was sent home, Forge transferred to a new post, and his letters to Gage went unanswered.

Now in the middle of a bitter divorce, Forge is sick and tired of his husband's manipulation. He's almost ready to make *any* sacrifice to get closure—then he finds Granger murdered execution-style in their home. Forge had no idea about Granger's illicit activities, but the killers don't believe that. They think Forge has something they want, and they're coming after him.

When Forge's lawyer arranges for professional protection, the last face Forge expects to see is Gage's. Can he even contemplate a second chance for them after almost two decades, or will hoping only lead to more heartache? Before they can explore the possibilities, they must figure out what information Granger had—that others are willing to kill for—or that possible heartache could become a certainty.

www.dreamspinnerpress.com

LOST MATE
DIRK GREYSON

Wolf shifter Falco Gladstone knew Carter McCloud was his mate when they were in seventh grade, but school and the foster care system tore them apart. Years later, Falco is second in command of his Michigan pack, serving under an uncle who cares more about his own power than the welfare of their people. The alpha orders Falco to marry and produce offspring—but Falco's already found his mate, and mates are forever.

Carter's lonely life is turned upside down when he detects a familiar scent on the wind. The mates might have found each other, but their happily ever after is far from guaranteed. Falco's commitment to Carter puts him at odds with his uncle's plans, and when one of the alpha's enforcers starts shadowing the couple, something must be done—something that will either cement their relationship or destroy it once and for all.

www.dreamspinnerpress.com

PLAYING
WITH
FIRE

DIRK GREYSON

Jim Crawford was born wealthy, but he turned his back on it to become a police officer. Add that to his being gay, and he's definitely the black sheep of the family.

Dr. Barty Halloran grew up with lessons instead of friends and toys and as a result, became a gifted psychologist… with only an academic understanding of people and emotions.

When Jim's pursuit of a serial killer goes nowhere, he turns to Dr. Halloran for help, and Barty thinks he can get inside the shooter's mind. In many ways, they're two sides of the same coin, which both scares and intrigues him. Together, Jim and Barty make progress on the case—until the stakes shoot higher when the killer turns his attention toward Barty.

To protect Barty, Jim offers to let Barty stay with him, where he discovers the doctor has a heart to go along with his brilliant mind after all. But as they close in on their suspect, the killer becomes desperate, and he'll do anything to elude capture—even threaten those closest to Jim.

www.dreamspinnerpress.com

FLIGHT OR FIGHT

DIRK GREYSON

Life in the big city wasn't what Mackenzie "Mack" Redford expected, and now he's come home to Hartwick County, South Dakota, to serve as sheriff.

Brantley Calderone is looking for a new life. After leaving New York and buying a ranch, he's settling in and getting used to living at a different pace—until he finds a dead woman on his porch and himself the prime suspect in her murder.

Mack and Brantley quickly realize several things: someone is trying to frame Brantley; he is no longer safe alone on his ranch; and there's a definite attraction developing between them, one that only increases when Mack offers to let Brantley stay in his home. But as their romance escalates, so does the killer. They'll have to stay one step ahead and figure out who wants Brantley dead before it's too late. Only then can they start the life they're both seeking—together.

www.dreamspinnerpress.com